SAVIOR

UNDERCOVER

BOOK THREE

USA TODAY BESTSELLING AUTHOR

HEATHER SLADE

MORE FROM AUTHOR HEATHER SLADE

BUTLER RANCH
Kade's Worth
Brodie's Promise
Maddox's Truce
Naughton's Secret
Mercer's Vow
Kade's Return
Butler Ranch Christmas

WICKED WINEMAKERS
FIRST LABEL
Brix's Bid
Ridge's Release
Press' Passion
Zin's Sins
Tryst's Temptation

WICKED WINEMAKERS
SECOND LABEL
Beau's Beloved
Cru's Crush
Bit's Bliss
Coming Soon:
Snapper's Seduction
Kick's Kiss

ROARING FORK RANCH
Roaring Fork Wrangler
Coming Soon:
Roaring Fork Roughstock
Roaring Fork Rockstar
Roaring Fork Rooker
Roaring Fork Bridger

THE ROYAL AGENTS
OF MI6
Make Me Shiver
Drive Me Wilder
Feel My Pinch
Chase My Shadow
Find My Angel

K19 SECURITY
SOLUTIONS TEAM ONE
Razor's Edge
Gunner's Redemption
Mistletoe's Magic
Mantis' Desire
Dutch's Salvation

K19 SECURITY
SOLUTIONS TEAM TWO
Striker's Choice
Monk's Fire
Halo's Oath
Tackle's Honor
Onyx's Awakening

K19 SHADOW OPERATIONS
TEAM ONE
Code Name: Ranger
Code Name: Diesel
Code Name: Wasp
Code Name: Cowboy
Code Name: Mayhem

K19 ALLIED INTELLIGENCE
TEAM ONE
Code Name: Ares
Code Name: Cayman
Code Name: Poseidon
Code Name: Zeppelin
Code Name: Magnet

K19 ALLIED INTELLIGENCE
TEAM TWO
Code Name: Puck
Code Name: Michelangelo
Code Name: Typhon
Coming Soon:
Code Name: Hornet
Code Name: Reaper

PROTECTORS
UNDERCOVER
Undercover Agent
Undercover Emissary
Undercover Savior
Coming Soon:
Undercover Infidel
Undercover Assassin

THE INVINCIBLES
TEAM ONE
Code Name: Deck
Code Name: Edge
Code Name: Grinder
Code Name: Rile
Code Name: Smoke

THE INVINCIBLES
TEAM TWO
Code Name: Buck
Code Name: Irish
Code Name: Saint
Code Name: Hammer
Code Name: Rip

THE UNSTOPPABLES
TEAM ONE
Code Name: Fury
Code Name: Merried
Coming Soon:
Code Name: Vex
Code Name: Steel
Code Name: Jagger

COWBOYS OF
CRESTED BUTTE
A Cowboy Falls
A Cowboy's Dance
A Cowboy's Kiss
A Cowboy Stays
A Cowboy Wins

Table of Contents

1

Sullivan

There was a chance I'd win a Pulitzer for the story I'd been working on for the last six months, but I didn't care about that. Exposing Eric Weber as the *boggen minger*—foul-smelling scumbag—he was, motivated me far more than accolades ever would.

Tomorrow, the Edinburgh offices of the Crown Herald News Agency, the UK's most trusted investigative news organization and my employer, would lock up for the holidays for all but late-breaking news stories. Which meant I'd no longer have access to some of the more secure servers I relied on for my research, at least until after the beginning of the new year.

I'd make do, of course, since the current story I was working on required me to find and cultivate my own sources—ones I had no intention of revealing, let alone sharing, even within my department.

Given I'd spent the day attempting to come up with every conceivable thing I might need to use the classified servers to find, my desk, that my editor typically referred to as a "muddle of epic proportions," was worse than usual.

Scraps of paper where I'd jotted down random thoughts to follow up on were buried under days-old cups containing no-longer-discernible beverages. That I didn't give a fuck was only one reason my colleagues, which was far too nice a word to call them, avoided my corner of the office. Actually, my untidiness was what had landed me at the desk shoved off in a windowless alcove.

That, along with my tenacity, had earned me the nickname bulldog. I was more often called Bully than Sully—short for my first name, Sullivan—not that the two rhymed. It was meant to be insulting, but I considered it high praise.

"Rivers, my office, now," barked Clive Edwards, executive editor of investigations, as well as a former recipient of the prestigious Pulitzer. He was also my mother's brother. Before I was hired for my current position, he'd made the importance of us concealing our relationship clear.

Given he headed up the investigations team, I doubted we'd be successful in keeping the secret for very long. That my coworkers still hadn't figured out I was related to the boss spoke volumes about the caliber of reporters most of them were.

Had they discovered the truth, they wouldn't have been able to cry nepotism at my rapid climb within the department; it certainly hadn't been because of my uncle. He wasn't responsible for my getting the job, in the first place, nor did he cut me any slack. I'd gotten where I was by being the bulldog I'd come to be known as.

"Yes, sir," I muttered at his command, digging around for a notepad and pen, and racing into his office before the door shut in my face.

"Where are you with the Tower-Meridian investigation?"

"Getting close, sir."

He raised a brow. "That's hardly an answer, and you know it." He leaned back in his chair and looked out at the view of Edinburgh Castle afforded by his corner office. "I received a message from the higher-ups."

My eyes scrunched as I processed what such a statement could mean. "Regarding?"

"They're pulling the plug on the story."

My eyes practically bulged out of my head. I'd dedicated the last several months of my life to this investigation to the exclusion of nearly everything else. I couldn't fathom being forced to quit now when I truly was close. "You can't be serious."

"I am. The new editor in chief, Fallon Wallace, is taking a close look at each department's budget and making significant cuts. We won't be able to fund the kind of expenses we have in the past."

"Understood. I'll rein in expenditures."

He turned his chair to face me. "That isn't all."

"Go on."

"The news agency has received threats."

I raised a brow. "Can you be more specific?"

"We kill the story, or you suffer the same fate."

"Someone wants me dead?" If there were ever a threat that would achieve the exact opposite response than intended, it was this. It nearly made me giddy. "I'm closer than I thought," I said under my breath.

"This is no laughing matter, Sullivan."

"Look, what kind of investigative journalist would I be if a death threat deterred me?"

"A living one. Your mother made me promise—"

"Please don't," I whispered. I'd spent my entire life defending my inquisitive nature to my mum, starting as far back as I could remember.

"Your teacher complains that you disrupt his lessons with your constant questions," she'd said after returning from a conference with the man. "It's bad enough that we have to endure it here, at home."

While I didn't remember his exact words, my father had probably muttered something about letting me be before returning to the book he was reading.

I couldn't recall a single time I'd seen him without a tome in his hand or at least close by. I supposed I'd inherited his quest for knowledge, albeit with a different approach. I was an incessant question asker while he read voraciously.

"When we return from the holiday break, you'll either be assigned something else, or if you don't let this go, you'll be fired."

"But—"

"The decision is final. Am I making myself clear?"

"Yes, sir," I responded.

I stood and walked out of his office, my mind reeling from the edict. The only thing I knew for sure was I had no intention of following orders. If not to the Crown Herald, I'd eventually sell the story to someone else.

As I slowly made my way to my desk, I glanced around, realizing that, in the short time I was in Clive's office, everyone else had cleared out early without as much as wishing me a pleasant holiday. It didn't matter. There wasn't a single person in this department, or any other at the Crown Herald, who I considered a friend.

I cleaned up the worst of the trash cluttering my workspace, shoving the random scraps of paper into my computer bag and smashing them down in the bottom by jamming my laptop in the same compartment. I was about to turn my desktop PC off when an alert popped up on the screen.

"Eric Weber, infamous and elusive CEO of Tower-Meridian Consolidated, is rumored to be making a rare public appearance at this evening's fundraiser at Edinburgh Castle," read the message on my screen. Tonight, I would finally come face-to-face with the man who'd managed to keep his likeness out of the press to the point where neither I nor anyone else I'd spoken with had any idea what he looked like.

I glanced over my shoulder to make sure Clive was still in his office, then dug through my desk drawer, frantically searching for my press badge. I'd so rarely used it that I wondered if it was even current.

"Yes!" I nearly shouted when I found it beneath several file folders and what looked like a moldy piece of cardboard that had probably started out as pizza. I dumped it and the paper plate it was stuck to in the rubbish bin, grabbed my coat, and stuffed the badge and lanyard in my pocket. I was about to rap on my uncle's door to wish him a happy Christmas when I heard him on the phone. "I've done all I can. The rest is in your hands now," I heard him say. I eased away from the door and had just reached the lift when I heard him shout my name.

I hit the call button and spun around. "Good night, sir," I said, ducking in as soon as the door opened. I leaned up against the back wall and thought about what I'd overheard. Had he been speaking with my mum? Was the death threat a fabrication meant to scare me enough that I'd abandon my investigation? Surely, he wouldn't have gone that far just to appease my mother's worry. But then why would he have said the rest was in "your hands now"? He had to have been talking to someone else and not about me at all.

Once home, I scoured the internet for whatever I could find about the event taking place later that night.

"Young People's Trust," I muttered in disgust, reading the list of charities the fundraiser supported. That a man I was certain funded human and maybe even weapons trafficking would dare show his face at such an event sickened me.

While I had no intention of confronting him—What would I say if I did?—I certainly intended to make sure he knew I was there. And when I stared into his undoubtedly coal-black eyes, he'd see without any doubt that he didn't scare me. Not one bit.

The only drawback to going was that the event was black tie. I pulled the one gown I owned from the back of my closet, praying that it still fit and wasn't a wrinkled mess. I couldn't wear a bra with it, and it was too long to go without heels, which I'd also managed to find buried beneath several pairs of more practical footwear.

I'd spent thirty minutes searching for a place to leave my car before giving in and forking over the fifty pounds at the gate in order to park in the valet lot.

While waiting for the attendant to appear where I'd been instructed to proceed, I felt around inside my bag for my press badge. "Where in the bloody hell did it go?" I muttered just as another car pulled up closer to the castle's entrance and stopped. Given it was a limousine with darkened windows, there was at least a chance the person being transported was none other than the man I'd been investigating—Eric Weber.

Rather than continue waiting for the attendant, I eased the door open and got out. When the credential I'd been searching for, that had apparently been on my lap, fell to the ground, I knelt down to grab it. Seconds after I stood and brushed off my dress, I froze.

"You were warned," a man's voice said before he put his hand over my mouth, and the gun he held against my temple cocked.

The limousine sped off, leaving me alone with the person I was sure intended to kill me once it was far enough away. I always figured this would be the way I'd go—on the verge of the biggest story of my career, one that would take down a man as vile as I could imagine.

I held my breath, shut my eyes, and sighed. If this was how I'd die, I could at least take satisfaction in knowing I was right about the bloody bastard.

2

Savior

"There are two targets," said Periscope, my handler. "Your orders are to eliminate both."

"Who are they?" I asked as I exited my SUV and got into position.

"The first is Sullivan Rivers, a reporter with the Crown Herald. The second, the gunman, is yet to be identified."

Sullivan Rivers. Why did that name sound familiar? More, why had I asked who the victims were when I never had before? And a reporter? Why was there a hit order on her?

"Take the first shot as soon as you've got it," I heard Periscope say through my comms earpiece. Who the fuck did she think she was talking to? I was one of the best snipers in Unit 23, an elite team within SIS—the UK's Secret Intelligence Service—whose primary mission objective was assassination. And I wasn't one of the best—I was *the* best—and she damn well knew it. "Savior? Copy?"

"Shut the fuck up," I seethed, pulling the trigger the very instant I knew I'd hit the gunman right between the eyes. A quick *pfft* was all he heard. It might not even have registered. No audible crack since I only used subsonic bullets.

I was about to take the second shot when two things stopped me. First, I was sure I knew the woman whose life I was about to end. Second, I could see shadowy figures approaching from the edge of the parking lot where one victim lay dead on the ground and the other stood frozen and in shock.

"Bloody fucking hell," I muttered, slamming my foot on the gas after jumping into my waiting SUV and racing over to the woman, who was bent over, losing the contents of her stomach. I got out, grabbed her around the waist, and shoved her inside. I climbed in after her, barely getting the door closed before I spun my vehicle in the opposite direction and sped out of the parking lot.

"Get down on the floor!" I shouted. "Keep your hands where I can see them."

"Savior, *do you copy?*" I heard Periscope say through the comms.

"Copy," I responded.

"The cleanup crew is going in now. They're saying there's only one victim—the gunman." She sounded out of breath. "Where is the other target?"

"With me."

"What's going on, Savior?"

"I'll handle it," I said right before powering off my headset.

"Who the fuck are you?" asked the woman holding onto the seat as I careened from outside the castle gates through the streets of Edinburgh.

I didn't respond. My mind was still reeling from what I'd just done, acting entirely out of instinct.

Her name, Sullivan Rivers, was unique enough that when I heard it, I recognized it immediately. Then, when I looked through the scope and prepared to take the shot, I was certain she was the same girl whose pigtails I used to pull when we were in primary school. Our families had been neighbors for a brief time twenty years ago, when we spent a few months living in Ballater outside Balmoral Castle. While the time had been brief, I never forgot her.

Glancing in her direction now, our eyes met, and I knew I hadn't been wrong. The girl I used to call Sully was on the floor of my SUV rather than lying dead on a parking lot's pavement—and as soon as word of what I'd done got back to my boss, I'd be in a fuck of a lot of trouble.

I returned my eyes to the road but could feel her studying me. I hardly resembled the scrawny boy she'd once known, and my given name—David Evans—was commonplace enough that if I divulged what it was, I doubted she'd make the connection.

As for my appearance, my previously white-blond hair had turned darker, my body filled out, and rather than being a few inches shorter than her like I was then, I now had at least a foot on her.

The other thing that had changed between the last time she saw me and now was that my heart had turned black as coal. That's what happened to people in my line of work. It didn't matter that I rid the world of another piece-of-shit criminal with every bullet I fired. I shot to kill. Period. I'd lost track of my body count a long time ago.

And yet, they called me Savior. Tonight, it fit. I'd chosen to save Sullivan's life rather than take it. God knew what had possessed me to do it. I'd never disregarded a direct order. I was duty bound to assassinate those who posed a threat to the United Kingdom and its citizens.

Tonight, Sullivan River's life had been spared while the man who meant to kill her had suffered the fate. No doubt, in the coming days or weeks, I'd receive another assignment with the same anticipated outcome. It was, after all, what I was paid to do. That was if I still had a job.

"Can I get up now?" she asked.

"Not yet," I said, glancing down at the woman whose face had turned a putrid shade of green.

"Unless you have something I can empty the rest of the contents of my stomach into, you're going to regret making me wait."

We were now far enough away from the Royal Mile that I would've picked up on a tail. However, that didn't mean one wouldn't materialize.

"Stay put," I said, making another turn, this one unplanned.

"Is it really necessary for you to still have your hand on that gun?"

"Until I know you're unarmed, it absolutely is."

"Did you get a look at what I'm wearing? Where would I have a weapon?"

I pulled into the underground car park of a nondescript building owned by one of my closest friends, a man I knew I could trust to help me determine the next best course of action when I informed him of the split-second decision I'd made tonight.

When I didn't see his vehicle, I got out of mine and sent him a text, alerting him of my arrival, saying I had someone with me and I'd explain everything later.

When he responded immediately, acknowledging my message, I walked around to open her door.

"Wait, is this thing bulletproof?" she asked, putting her hand on the metal, which was at least twice as thick as normal. Once her feet were on the ground, I spun her around so her back was to me. "Hands on the side of the SUV," I barked.

"What are you doing?" she shrieked when I patted her down, looking for a gun.

"Do not move," I said, keeping my elbow pinned to her back and one foot between her legs as I sent an access code via my mobile.

"This way." I turned her around a second time, took her arm, and led her to a lift that opened when we approached.

"Where are you taking me? And you can put that thing down now," she said, motioning to the gun I still held pointed in her direction. "Are you going to answer any of my questions?" she asked when I lowered it.

"No." I glanced over at her when I felt her studying me. Our eyes met, and hers scrunched enough that I wondered if she recognized me. I passed the idea off as ludicrous while I waited for the door to reopen.

"Come with me," I said after we stepped off and into the flat that was always at my disposal but I rarely used.

"How long will we be here? I need to go back and get my car."

I almost rolled my eyes at the ridiculousness of Sullivan's question. Was she truly unaware of how close she'd come to dying tonight? Not once, but twice.

"Sit down, and do not touch anything."

When she raised her chin and her eyes met mine, the only thing I could think of was how much I wanted to wrap my fingers around her throat and kiss the fuck out of her. Instead, I kept my hands to myself when I stepped closer.

"You would do well to consider the fact I saved your life earlier tonight, first by shooting the man who was about to do the same to you, then getting you away from there before someone else took you out. If you do not do as I say, I will honor your request to return you to your vehicle. Once there, I guarantee you will not like what happens next."

Her expression remained defiant. "Are you threatening me?"

"I'm warning you."

"If you're going to kill me, why not just do it here? Why return me to the scene of the other crime?"

"Because I won't be the one who kills you. I also won't save you a second time. I have a couple of calls to make. Now, get over here and sit down."

When she did, I stood behind her, pulled my belt through the loops of my trousers, and used it to bind her wrists to the chair.

I took my mobile from my pocket, stepped into one of the bedrooms, and closed the door behind me. There were several missed calls from Periscope, but only one from Typhon, my boss.

"Savior, what the fuck is going on?" he seethed when he accepted my call.

"Who ordered the hit tonight?"

"It came through MI6."

"From who?" I demanded.

"Settle down and tell me what happened."

"Not until you tell me who the order came from."

He sighed. "Initially, it was reported to have come from Viper. However, I've spoken with her and she insisted she didn't issue it."

I paced from one side of the room to the other.

"Tell me what went down," he pressed.

"I arrived on the scene and didn't carry out the full order. I made a split-second decision to remove the second intended target from the area."

"After my conversation with Viper, I believe you made the right call."

"Where is Periscope?"

"On her way to headquarters."

I'd worked with her for just over a year and had a hard time believing she would issue an erroneous order. "Who is she saying it came from?"

"That's presently unclear, but I anticipate it won't be much longer. Where are you now?" he asked.

"Still in Edinburgh, not far from the castle."

"I'm going to request something of you that I know is out of the ordinary. Can you protect the asset until I know exactly what happened tonight and what the fallout might be?"

"Yes, sir." I'd already made the decision to—one way or another—so I had no reason to argue.

"Good and thank you. I'll get to the bottom of this as quickly as I can. In the meantime, do not act on any order that doesn't come directly from me."

"Yes, sir," I repeated.

"And, while I anticipate you'll be getting help from the rest of your crew, no one outside of them and me is to be read in on your plan."

"Yes, sir," I responded for the third time.

"In the meantime, stay alive. You're needed here, Savior." Typhon ended with his customary sendoff to all the agents who worked for him in Unit 23.

The next call I made was to Conrad Carnegie, aka the Earl of Blackmoor, one of my most trusted friends and the man who owned the building where I'd brought Sullivan tonight.

"What in the bloody hell is going on, Ash?" He was chuckling when he answered.

"I'm not sure you'll believe me when I tell you."

"You're on speaker, by the way. Tag and Gus are both here."

While Con, Tag, Gus, and I had been friends since we were children, it wasn't until secondary school that we began using our nicknames. Con was short for Conrad, his first name. Same with Gus, for Angus. Tag was for MacTaggert, his last name. And even though my father was alive at the time I was given the moniker, they still called me Ash, as I was the *future* Duke of Ashcroft.

We all worked for Unit 23 in some capacity and made up the crew Typhon had referred to.

Tag, aka Niall MacTaggert, the Earl of Glenshadow, code name Obsidian, was an assassin, like I was.

Con was one of the preeminent cyber- and artificial-intelligence experts in all of SIS—maybe even the world.

The way Gus fit into our group was entirely different, but he was no less important. In fact, some might say he was the glue that held us all together.

Like me, he grew up on Ashcroft, but rather than an heir, he was the son of Mairi—pronounced

Mary—Drummond, who'd been our housekeeper for as long as I could remember.

Gus and I were inseparable as children, apart from the one year my parents and I spent in Ballater. The year I met Sullivan. When I returned, nothing had changed other than me losing my heart to a blue-eyed girl whose pigtails I'd loved to pull.

More than Con or Tag, Gus was forced to listen as I told stories of how amazing she was. It was hard to imagine now how such a young lad, as I was at the time, could be so enraptured. Perhaps, somewhere deep inside, I'd sensed the story wasn't over for Sullivan and me. Not by a long shot.

My father had arranged for Gus to attend university with me, and after graduation, we were recruited by SIS. He went to work for MI5, the domestic equivalent of MI6, where I'd landed.

Eventually, we both ended up at Unit 23. At first, he was a handler, but as his real skill set became more apparent to Typhon, he transitioned to being the team's eyes and ears in the west of Scotland, where Con and Tag also grew up.

His cover as butler at my family's estate, where he still resided, served him well in intelligence gathering. No one on the staff, with the exception of his mum, knew the vital role he played in carrying out his oath to the Crown. Even she had no idea the full extent of what he did.

"As you're all aware, I set out from London earlier in the day on my way to Ashcroft for the holidays. I'd just arrived within Edinburgh city limits when I received a call from Periscope, saying MI6 was asking for my support at the castle. Upon my arrival there, I was informed there were two targets. The first was a gunman who held the second with his gun to her head."

Now that I thought about it, it made no sense to call me in for *two* hit orders. Why wouldn't MI6 allow the gunman to kill the woman, then have me take him out? I shook my head, thankful that wasn't how it had gone down.

"The woman—and this is the part you won't believe—was Sullivan Rivers."

"No!" Con gasped. "Not *the* Miss Rivers."

Gus wasn't the only one who'd had to endure my stories. All three of my friends had heard ad nauseam about the then-eight-year-old girl who'd captured my heart.

"I couldn't do it," I admitted.

"Of course you couldn't," muttered Tag. "You're Savior, not Lucifer."

"Most times, I feel like the latter," I responded under my breath to the man I knew understood better than most others. I cleared my throat. "Most troubling right now is that it's unclear who issued the order."

"I've received a communication from Typhon on that subject," said Con.

I wasn't surprised. "I spoke with him a few minutes ago, and he requested that, until we can determine exactly what happened tonight and why, I be the one responsible for asset protection."

"Where is Sullivan now?" Con asked.

"In the other room." Which reminded me she was also bound to a chair. I couldn't leave her that way much longer.

"What's your plan?" Gus asked, no doubt already anticipating my response.

"To bring her with me to Ashcroft. It'll be the easiest place to keep her safe."

This pertained to him more than the others, given his mother's position at the estate.

"One hiccup," he said. "My mum informed me earlier that Brose arrived today and plans to remain through the first of the year."

Ambrose Ashcroft, who insisted everyone call him Brose as Gus had, was my father's younger brother and the bane of my dad's existence when he was still alive. While he claimed to make a living as an international art dealer and collector, I knew that, prior to my becoming duke, Brose received an extravagant allowance from the estate. Thankfully, my father had set up an irrevocable trust to continue his brother's annual stipend, saving me from having to dole it out, as well as a potential argument about an increase.

The man was more a doddering nuisance than a threat. However, I wouldn't risk exposing Sullivan to him.

"You could stay in the cottage until we can figure out a compelling-enough reason to get Brose to leave," Gus suggested.

"The *one-bedroom* cottage?"

"Look at it this way, Ash. Your childhood fantasy is finally becoming reality," joked Con.

I didn't laugh. His suggestion reminded me that Sullivan was currently wearing a red, sexy-as-fuck gall gown. "One other thing. She'll need clothing and, err, incidentals."

"I'll have it taken care of," said Gus.

"It needs to be tonight."

"Understood, Ash."

At that very moment, I heard the woman screech, followed by what sounded like the chair toppling over.

"Gotta run, gents," I said before ending the call and racing from the room.

3

Sullivan

"Ow," I groaned when the side of my head hit the floor. Thankfully, there was a plush rug under the chair that had tipped over when I tried to tug my hands free.

"Sullivan!" The man whose name I didn't know despite him knowing mine came rushing down the hallway.

He removed the belt from my wrists, then lifted me into his arms. Rather than right the chair, he carried me over to the sofa.

"Are you hurt anywhere?" he asked, stroking my hair with one hand while keeping me on his lap with the opposite arm.

"Who are you?" I asked, looking into eyes that were so familiar yet I couldn't place where I'd seen them before.

He sighed, shifted me off his lap, and stood. "I'll explain later. For now, we need to be on our way."

When he held out his hand, I considered refusing, but what would I do? I had no idea where I was other than somewhere in Edinburgh. I'd left everything in my car, so I had no means to call someone to pick me up, and even if I was able to contact a car service, I was dressed in little more than a ball gown and heels. Considering the night I'd had, I was disheveled, had been sick to my stomach more than once, and was sure the little makeup I wore was in streaks on my cheeks from crying. Not that I'd done it in front of him.

As soon as he'd left me bound to the chair, a torrent of tears fell from my eyes. The sobs racking my body were silent; I'd always been a quiet crier, even as a baby.

I looked up into the stranger's eyes and took his outstretched hand. "Will you at least tell me your name?"

"David," he said, removing the Harris Tweed jacket he wore. "Here, put this on."

I eased my arms, one of which was already sore, into the sleeves.

"Let's go. We have a long drive ahead of us." He led me to the door and out to the lift.

"Where are you taking me?"

"Somewhere you'll be safe."

"Thank you, David," I said to the man who… What was he? My savior? Guardian? Protector? There was also a chance he might be my killer, given one man had already met the same fate tonight. Plus, it seemed like he didn't like me very much.

If I was in danger, I had to admit there was a certain comfort knowing I was being transported in an armored vehicle.

"My colleague is making arrangements for clothing and other incidentals to be delivered to the place where you'll be staying."

Clothing and incidentals? Okay. That seemed odd. How did the colleague know what size I wore? And, by the latter, did he mean things like knickers? God, I'd be mortified if that was the case.

"Wait. I need my computer and my mobile."

David glanced in my direction. "Not possible."

I shook my head. "I'm serious. I can't leave it in my car, where anyone might get their hands on it. Do you understand what I'm saying?"

"I presume your work is stored on some kind of cloud-based server, is it not?"

"Not entirely." Especially not anymore, given the last thing I did before leaving the office was download every last piece of research I'd collected from the servers onto my laptop. I'd also deleted it, not that anyone working for the Crown Herald couldn't have retrieved it.

I hadn't spent an hour in this man's presence, yet I was already familiar with the *exasperated* look he gave me. "Can't your colleague make arrangements for that to be delivered as well?" I wasn't crazy about the idea, but given David had said if he did honor my request to return me to my vehicle, I would likely be killed, I thought better of pressing him to do it.

"Well?" I asked when he didn't respond.

"As I already said, retrieving your computer or your mobile will not be possible."

"Wait a minute. Whoever you work for already has them, don't they? They're scrubbing them for everything they can get their grimy hands on."

He raised a brow at my disparaging word choice. "Err, present company excluded from the grimy comment."

He sighed and glanced over at me like I was a speck of lint he'd like to brush off his jacket. "I doubt the people I work for would find anything on them they don't already know."

"I can't just leave it there."

"'No' was never a word you accepted without an argument," he said under his breath.

"What does that mean? And more, how would you know?"

"It was a supposition."

"By the way, I have exceptional hearing."

"Noted." He wriggled in his seat.

"Is something wrong?"

"I'm hungry."

He sounded so much like a little boy that I nearly giggled. Or I would have if the memory of a gun being pressed against my temple was more distant. "You could've shot me."

David shook his head. "I could have done. I chose not to."

My mouth gaped. "What does that mean?" I asked for the second time. "Are you saying I was supposed to die? Is that what this car ride is all about? You're taking me somewhere to kill me? Somewhere remote where my body will never be discovered?"

"Perhaps you should've considered a career as a fiction writer over investigative journalism."

"Can we *please* go get my computer?" I pleaded. "I'm begging now."

In anticipation of another negative response, I struggled to come up with a reason it would be imperative we do so. Instead, I was stunned when David touched his ear, then began talking.

"That's right. See to it everything in the vehicle is removed, boxed up, and delivered."

Everything? Would whoever he was talking to be able to discern what might be considered rubbish? "Err…"

He glanced over at me. "What now?"

"Just the computer and mobile will be fine. Thanks."

He didn't respond, nor did he say anything else to the person he'd asked to gather my things.

"We can stop somewhere if you're hungry," I said when I saw him rub his stomach.

"Not a good idea."

"Wouldn't you know by now if someone was following us?"

He shot me the exasperated look again.

"It's a valid question," I said under my breath.

"You aren't the only one with exceptional hearing."

Considering the mess my life was at the moment, that anything could make me smile stunned me.

While he drove, I sneaked glances at him. Weirdly, more than his eyes seemed familiar, but I still couldn't place him.

"Do you live in Edinburgh?" I asked.

"No."

"London?"

"Do you ever stop asking questions? Wait. I already know the answer."

"You do?"

He smirked.

"So, do you live in London?"

"I have a place there. Not that I'm there very often."

"Where are you instead?"

David glanced over at me again and shook his head. "Not there."

"The place where you're taking me?" I asked.

"I'm there even less."

While he didn't sound sad while talking about it, I couldn't help but think the life he led was. I was about to ask about his family when I thought of mine. "I need to check in with my parents." I waited several seconds for him to respond. "Did you hear me?" I finally asked.

"Someone will get word to them that you're safe."

My mouth gaped. "What does that mean?" I asked for what had to be the third or fourth time.

"You will not be permitted contact with anyone."

I was about to ask if that included using my computer, but thought better of it. Surely, once I had it, I'd be able to send a secure message.

"Whatever you're thinking, forget it. Someone tried to kill you tonight, Sullivan, and it wasn't because you happened to be at the wrong place at the wrong time. They knew you were coming."

"Did you?" I asked.

He shook his head. "I did not."

"Did the people you work for?"

He shot me the look. "One would think a decent investigative reporter would know the answer without needing to ask the question."

"'A decent investigative reporter would know the answer,'" I mimicked, facing the passenger window and resting my head against the seat.

How ironic was it that I was close enough to discovering the truth about Eric Weber, and yet now I had to choose between pursuing the rest of the story and sur-viving? Earlier tonight, I'd had a gun against my head. When I was growing up in Ballater, the village outside Balmoral Castle, I couldn't say such a thing would've ever entered my mind.

"David, where did you grow up?" I asked. Something about my childhood hometown made me wonder about his.

"My family moved quite often."

"Edinburgh?"

"No. I spent more time in the west of Scotland."

I was stunned he'd admitted that much. As long as he was talkative…

"Why were you at the charity event tonight?"

"In part because the people I work for received intel you would be." The muscle at the corner of his right eye twitched.

"How? I mean, how could they know?"

"Think, Sullivan. Many of the questions you've asked me, you already know the answer to."

"Do you work for SIS?" I asked.

He shot me the look *again*.

Since that seemed obvious, if they knew I planned to be there, they hadn't found out via a guest list. The only way they could've was by hacking into my computer, surveilling me, or they'd been the ones to send the alert that Eric Weber would be in attendance. All notions rattled me. Maybe I was in too deep. I was a lone reporter, albeit one with access to the Crown Herald's data banks and a wide network of sources. SIS would have exponentially more, along with access to intelligence the news agency never would. Oh, and they had snipers available on demand, not something a news agency could claim.

If I gave up now, would Eric Weber and his accomplices ever face judgment? I shook my head. I *couldn't* quit, not in good conscience. It didn't matter if the people I worked for buried the story. I'd find someone else interested in running it.

I decided to bite the bullet and ask if I'd be allowed to work where we were going. "You said I wouldn't be permitted to contact anyone."

He may have nodded. I wasn't certain.

I bit my bottom lip. "What about work?"

"Your offices are closed for the holidays."

"I can continue working on my story whether the Crown Herald is open or not."

David took in a deep breath and let it out slowly. "Someone wants to kill you, Sullivan. More than one entity, in fact. It's my job to ensure whoever it is, or they are, they don't find out."

"What about research?"

I wasn't surprised when he didn't respond.

Even if I figured out a way to send a secure message, other than my parents, who would I contact? Clive? I thought about the conversation I'd overheard. Rather than speaking with my mother as I'd assumed, what if he was alerting the people who'd wanted to kill me? The idea that my uncle would do such a thing sickened me.

So, what were my options? I could continue pursuing the investigation on my own as I'd intended after Clive said he was *killing* it. Or I could let it go. That idea turned my stomach as much as thinking my uncle had betrayed me.

He'd said that after the holiday break, I'd be given a new assignment. Would I go back to where I started out, as a society reporter?

It was at an event I'd been requested to cover in that role where I'd overheard two people discussing Eric Weber's billion-dollar donation. After one said he'd hoped to finally get a glimpse of the man that evening, followed by the other saying Weber wouldn't dare show his face, my curiosity had kicked in and I began what would be the biggest investigation of my career. One that had led to my eventual promotion to the bureau where my uncle was executive editor.

So, what all was at play here? Were Weber and SIS on the same side?

"You said you chose not to kill me."

His glance in my direction told me he'd heard me.

"Why would SIS want me dead?"

Again, he didn't respond. However, I had a more pressing issue. "I need to use the loo."

"Can you wait another five minutes?"

It was questionable, but I said I could anyway.

David took the next exit from the highway, made several turns, then pulled up to a place that didn't look open.

He got out of the SUV, but when I tried to do the same, I discovered the door wouldn't budge. It opened for him, though.

"Do you use this vehicle for prisoner transport?" I asked.

No response. Not even the look.

"Didn't your parents teach you it's impolite to ignore someone speaking to you?"

"About as much as yours taught you it's rude to ask endless questions."

He rapped on a door marked "deliveries only," and seconds later, it opened.

"Welcome, your—" a man with a heavy Indian accent began, but stopped abruptly when David shook his head. "Table for two?" he asked instead.

"Please, Ramesh."

Rather than motioning for me to go first like any gentleman would, David followed the man who'd greeted us, giving me the opportunity to take him in from behind.

The view was breathtaking. Broad shoulders tapered in a V-shape to an arse any woman would want to get her hands on. I guessed he had to be six feet four, at least. And while I hadn't seen much of his face other than by the glow of the SUV's dashboard, it was enough to notice he was definitely handsome in a chiseled-Roman-god sort of way.

His aura, though, was what drew my attention the most. The way he carried himself portrayed a level of self-confidence bordering on arrogance—not something I usually found attractive.

The man was a sniper, worked for SIS, was broody in a typically Scottish way, had an amazing body, and once or twice, let his guard down enough for me to believe he had a dry wit.

It had been a while since I had a shag, good or bad, and I'd be willing to bet David would be an outstanding fuck.

As irritated as he seemed to be with me, I doubted that would be a perk of being under his protection.

4

Savior

If I were Sullivan, I'd ask an equal number of questions. On the other hand, not knowing my fate, I'd be more likely to remain mute in an effort to refrain from letting on anything I shouldn't.

"This is much appreciated," I said when Ramesh seated us at a table in the kitchen. It didn't appear there were many people in the dining room, but where we were, we wouldn't be seen should someone enter, looking for us.

"I've never eaten where I could see the chef preparing my food," Sullivan said after taking her seat in the chair I held out for her.

"Consider yourself lucky they aren't butchering anything tonight."

Her eyes widened, and I remembered her saying she needed to use the ladies' room.

"Come with me," I said before pushing her chair in. I led her to the restrooms, but before permitting her entry, I checked the one-room loo, which like the men's room, had no windows. "Go ahead," I added, stepping out.

I heard the click of the lock but remained right outside anyway. It had been a long time since I worked in witness protection, and when I had, the instances were few and far between. Still, much of it merely required common sense.

While waiting, I sent Gus a text, alerting him we'd stopped.

He responded almost immediately, saying the cottage on Eilean Mòr Ashcroft, an island that was part of my family's estate, was ready for our arrival and that he'd been able to arrange for the delivery of several items of clothing and other incidentals.

He also said Con had made arrangements for the contents of Sullivan's vehicle to be collected and delivered and that Typhon had approved the request.

Copy that, I responded. *Many thanks.*

Tomorrow, Gus, Con, and I would discuss the security measures we'd need to put in place both for Sullivan's protection against external threats as well as internal safeguards. Once she had her computer, it would be interesting to see how far she'd attempt to push her online activity. Everything would obviously be monitored and intercepted as necessary. What I needed to know more than anything was whether she could be trusted. My instincts told me she couldn't be. It was one time it would be nice to be proven wrong.

While staying in the cottage would delay my needing to make a decision, soon I'd have to address how much Sullivan would be permitted to learn about my family. Specifically—my title. Not only mine, but Con's and Tag's as well.

It was my work for Unit 23 that necessitated maintaining as much anonymity as possible, something that was controlled relentlessly both by SIS—the UK's Secret Intelligence Service—and by Con. In fact, he was far more adept at keeping all of us anonymous virtually.

To say he pushed the envelope of what was allowed in his role in intelligence was an understatement that had earned him the code name Infidel early in our careers.

When I heard the toilet flush and water running on the other side of the door, I shoved my mobile in my pocket.

Sullivan gasped when she came face-to-face with me after exiting the ladies' room.

"My apologies," I muttered, motioning for her to go ahead of me.

On our way to the kitchen, my hand hovered over the small of her back. Lord, how I wanted to rest it where her gown dipped, exposing her bare skin. Instead, I lowered it to my side and clenched my fist. With all that had happened in the last couple of hours, what kind of a wanker did fantasizing about touching Sullivan's naked body make me?

Ramesh had set a plate of papadams, green curry sauce, and samosas on the table and kindly held Sullivan's chair for her while I took my seat after she had.

"Something to drink?" he asked. "A Kingfisher, perhaps?"

"Go ahead," I said when Sullivan's eyes met mine. "Still water for me," I added before our host walked away.

"You seem so familiar to me."

When I didn't respond, she made a face.

"What? Should I have said you don't?" I asked.

"It would have been less rude than ignoring me."

I cocked my head. "Would it have?"

She took a bite of the samosa she'd put on her plate, closed her eyes, and uttered a sigh of pleasure. "This is fantastic," she said before taking a second bite.

Rather than partake myself, I watched her. Memories of a night when our families had dined *al fresco* on a perfect summer night floated back to me. My mum, who was a brilliant cook, had made one of our favorites—slow-roasted salmon. Sullivan's mother, whose first name I couldn't recall, had brought a dish of rumbledethumps—a traditional Scottish dish made of potato, cabbage, and onion. I knew there'd been other food served, but like Sullivan's mother's first name, I had no recollection of it.

What I remembered most was how much Sullivan loved the salmon, something she hadn't had before.

I didn't remember much about the house we'd lived in for that brief time, only that when we moved, I missed Sullivan more than anything else.

Now, I wanted to know everything about her life since we'd last seen each other, and I didn't want to read it in a dossier. I could guess what had made her pursue a career in journalism. Even at eight years old, she was the most inquisitive person I'd ever met.

When she'd said I seemed familiar to her, I was on the verge of asking if she recalled living next door to a skinny, scrawny boy, small for his age, who went by Davy. I'd stopped myself, knowing the risk of exposing who I was in society and what I did for a living was far too great. Years of covert work, of concealing who I was, of carrying out assignments around the world while maintaining my anonymity, couldn't be tossed aside just to share a pleasant memory with a childhood friend.

I'd made a vow to serve the Crown, and it would forever come before my personal desires.

It would become increasingly more difficult to keep up the lies I now avoided telling her simply by not responding.

The best thing for both of us would be for Typhon to determine who'd ordered the hit on Sullivan, assess the remaining threat, and make arrangements for her to be put in longer-term protective custody. I could walk away without revealing a thing about myself, and like that childhood crush, Sullivan Rivers would remain the stuff of fantasies.

Until such time as I heard from him, though, my options were to continue refusing to answer her questions, or I could come clean about who I was and admit she wasn't wrong about my familiarity. My final option was ensconcing her with either Tag or Con at their estates rather than at my own. Neither shared history with her, and both had alternate accommodations larger than I had at Ashcroft, even though my estate was greater in size.

Since I wasn't there often, unlike the two of them, who lived in the west of Scotland close to year-round, I kept a very small staff. Given most of them lived in the castle itself or in the village of Tarbert, there hadn't been a need to maintain or restore any of the older dwellings. Those that were inhabitable were occupied by tenants who'd lived in them for years.

There was one exception to my decision not to refurbish them. A few months ago, Gus had suggested the cottage that sat closest to the loch be rehabbed. I'd given my approval for it to be without bothering to ask why he made the request.

Now, though, I was curious. Perhaps his plan was to live in it, and that would be fine with me. Once I was no longer responsible for Sullivan's protection, I had every intention of resuming my life exactly as it had been, which meant it might be a year before I returned to Ashcroft again.

I'd never desired to live there full time like Con and Tag did on their estates.

Con, especially, loved spending most of his days in this part of Scotland. He entertained lavishly, hosting house parties similar to those our ancestors did a couple of centuries ago, requiring a far larger staff than I did.

Tag was happy here too, and when he wasn't on assignment for Unit 23, he was the epitome of a country squire. His familial home was a former monastery, and he raised prize-winning Highland cattle.

While I'd momentarily entertained the idea of Sullivan staying on one of their estates, her spending time with either man filled me with trepidation. Both were handsome, rugged, personable, and wealthy. Not that I thought the latter would matter to Sullivan. Still, what if she fell in love with Con or Tag? What if either of them felt the same for her? The thought of it made my chest tighten.

"I thought you were hungry," she said, motioning to the uneaten food on my plate.

"Famished," I muttered, digging into what was some of my favorite food.

"How did you find this place?" she asked while we waited for our entrees to be served.

"It was recommended." It was an accurate enough response. Ramesh Sharma's oldest son was a fellow Unit 23-er and someone I considered a friend. "Eat up. We still have a long drive ahead of us," I reminded her when dishes I hadn't ordered but the owner knew were my favorite were brought to the table.

"Where are we going?" Sullivan asked once we were in the SUV and back on the highway.

"Somewhere you'll be protected," I repeated the words I'd said previously when she asked. "Sleep if you're tired," I added when I saw her jar herself awake when her head drooped. She shifted her body so she could rest her head against the seat.

"It reclines if you'd be more comfortable."

She opened one eye. "Thank you for saving my life, David."

5

Sullivan

"We're here," I heard a voice say.

I opened my eyes and bolted upright, trying to figure out where I was. "Right," I said, looking into the darkness. "And where is here, exactly?" When he smirked, I remembered one of the last things he'd said before I drifted to sleep was that he was taking me somewhere I'd be protected, which also meant he didn't intend to tell me where it was then or now.

"The items I mentioned previously are already inside with the exception of what was in your car. I anticipate those will be by morning." He got out, came around, and opened my door. "My cottage is just over here." He held my arm as he led me on the uneven terrain. While I couldn't see much, I knew we were near water. I glanced up at a foreboding-looking castle that sat above us on a promontory. I'd ask which one it was, since Scotland had so many, except I doubted David would tell me.

"Is this where you live?" I asked.

"I'm not here often."

"Once again, he avoids answering the question," I said under my breath.

He raised a brow, but I caught a glimpse of a smirk. Even that seemed familiar to me. Why?

When we reached the front door, he fumbled with his keys, then had trouble opening it. He went in first, which seemed to be about making sure wherever we were entering was safe rather than because of a lack of manners.

"The bedroom is the last door down the hallway. As I said, you'll find something more comfortable to wear to, err, bed."

I nearly laughed out loud at the way his cheeks flushed, but stopped myself. The times when he revealed himself to be more than someone tasked with killing the man who would've done the same to me were so few and far between. I'd not draw attention to them, knowing it would make him more guarded.

I looked around the small but cozy living room, kitchen, and dining area. There were two two-seater sofas that sat at right angles to each other and faced a fireplace that someone had lit before our arrival. Behind me was a small kitchen with a farmhouse sink and a four-burner cooktop with an oven beneath it, flanked by cupboards. At the farthest end, there were built-in bench seats with a table in the middle, similar to a booth in a restaurant. Unsurprisingly, it was immaculate everywhere I looked.

Something dawned on me. "Did you say 'the' bedroom? As in, there's only one?"

"Yes."

"Where are you sleeping?"

"Out here," he answered, motioning to the loveseats, neither of which were long enough for him to lie down.

"I can sleep there," I offered.

"No."

I shook my head. The man was as stubborn as he was taciturn. "Very well," I muttered, walking in the direction he'd indicated. Before entering the room, I glanced over my shoulder. He was looking for something and appeared perplexed. "Is anything wrong?" I asked.

"No," he repeated.

"Do you need a blanket and pillow?"

"I'll make do."

I shrugged and opened the door. Like the outer rooms, the bedroom was small but lovely. On the chest of drawers, I found a toothbrush, toothpaste, and other personal care items, along with a pair of pajamas that looked to be close to my size. Then I opened a door I correctly assumed was a closet. While the rod where clothes would hang was empty, I noticed a blanket and two pillows on the shelf above it. I reached up and pulled them down, then carried them to the living room.

"I found these," I said.

"Right. Thanks."

"Good night, then," I added when he still appeared distracted.

"Yes. Good night."

I returned to the bedroom, retrieved the toothbrush, toothpaste, and pajamas, and went to the loo. Back in the bedroom, I snuggled under the heavy quilt and blankets.

It took me quite a while to fall asleep, unlike in the SUV when I did almost as soon as we got on the road.

I had no idea what time it was when I was jarred awake.

"Sullivan, you're dreaming," I heard David say just as the man who'd held a gun to my head pulled the trigger. I opened my eyes and looked up into his. He was sitting on the edge of the bed. "You're okay," he said in a soft and soothing voice I hadn't heard him use before.

"Nightmare," I mumbled.

"Will you be able to go back to sleep?"

"I think so," I said, even though I doubted I would. Every time I shut my eyes, I saw the gunman holding me as if I were hovering above, looking down at us.

"Do you want to talk about it?"

His question threw me, more because he'd asked.

"No, but thanks."

David stood and walked toward the hallway. "I'm right out there if you change your mind."

I couldn't shake the feeling that I knew this man prior to him saving my life tonight. It made no sense, but I'd learned long ago to trust my instincts. It was what made me a better journalist. Maybe what I was experiencing was some kind of hero-savior complex. He'd saved my life, and that was why I felt so safe with him.

After he left, I tossed and turned, wishing I had a book to read. Tomorrow, I'd see if there were any in the cottage.

When I woke again, I got out of bed and opened the window curtains. It was close to dawn, and a morning mist shrouded the castle I remembered noticing last night. From here, it appeared a weathered, deep-silver-gray medieval fortress set on a rocky promontory above what I guessed was a loch. Its multiple towers pierced the low morning clouds.

I wondered if it, like so many of those in Scotland, was open for public tours. And if not, whether David would be permitted to give me a private viewing.

After using the loo, I went out to the main rooms. "Hello?" I said when I didn't see David.

When there was no response, I peeked out a window to see if I could spot him. When I turned around, I noticed bags sitting on the floor. Taking a peek, I saw they were filled with women's clothes, most of which appeared to be my size.

I carried them into the bedroom, and when I found knickers and bras near the bottom, my cheeks flushed.

A silly reaction, given no one could see me. I pulled one of each out, along with a pair of trousers and a jumper, then carried them to the loo and took a shower.

When I returned to the main room and still didn't hear or see David, I put on a pair of socks and Wellies I found in another bag and grabbed a jacket that, like everything else, fit me as if it had been custom tailored.

I stepped outside and saw two people, a man and a woman, walking down the hillside toward a body of water. My suspicion that it was a loch was confirmed by the spit of land I could see in the distance on the opposite side.

From here, I couldn't tell if the man was David, so instead of following, I walked in the opposite direction, toward a bridge we must have driven over last night before he woke me. Once on the other side, I walked up a hill toward the castle.

"Good morning," said a man who came out of a side door when I approached. "You must be Sullivan."

"I am," I responded, stepping closer.

"I'm Angus Drummond." He bowed slightly at the waist. "May I help you with something?"

"I was looking for David, but when I couldn't find him, I decided to take a walk. Am I permitted to be up here?"

He smiled. "As long as you don't roam too far." He looked toward the water. "Here he is now."

"Good morning," David said, approaching us. A woman walked a few paces behind him.

"Sullivan, I'd like you to meet Mrs. Drummond."

The older woman bowed at the waist like the man who'd told me not to roam too far had. "It's a pleasure to meet you, miss, and please call me Mairi."

"Mrs. Drummond, err, Mairi takes care of the castle and other dwellings on the estate," said David. "Should you need anything, she will work her usual magic to ensure you get it."

The woman blushed and swatted David's arm with a familiarity I found endearing.

"On the off chance you're responsible for the clothing I found this morning, many thanks."

She smiled. "I am not, but as, err, David said, if you're in need of anything else, please let myself or Angus know."

Something occurred to me. "Wait. Mrs. Drummond and Angus Drummond?"

"Angus is my son," she responded, looking at him with obvious and endearing pride.

"The contents of your vehicle have been delivered." Angus motioned to an SUV parked behind us.

I caught a look pass between him and David right before the latter said he'd retrieve it and bring it to the cottage.

"By the way, the instructions were to bring *every-thing*," Angus said with a wink after David walked away.

I chuckled. "Most of what was found was likely rubbish."

"I can help you sort through it if you'd like," Mrs. Drummond offered. "As well as get you acquainted with the cottage."

While I didn't necessarily want her sifting through what was delivered, I wouldn't insult her by not taking her up on her offer. "That would be lovely. Thank you."

"Shall we?" She motioned to the pathway that led to the bridge that would take us to the cottage.

Neither of us spoke on the way, me because I was too busy taking in my surroundings. While well hidden, I still caught sight of surveillance cameras concealed in the stonework of the low walls surrounding the castle.

"The view is fabulous," I said, turning in a circle and picking up on the way the landscaping had been designed so there were clear lines of sight from all approaches, whether from where we came in last night or from the loch. No doubt the same was true for the forested land to the north and south of where we walked.

Regardless of how many centuries ago the castle had been built, it would have been designed as a fortress to protect against marauders. That explained its positioning on the promontory. However, the more modern technology I'd noticed was curious.

I hadn't been able to see it last night, but now, I noticed the lock on the cottage's door and the way Mrs. Drummond rested her hand on a pad where one might expect to see a doorbell. I heard a click, then she put the key in the lock and went inside ahead of me when it opened.

That level of security made some sense, knowing David was with SIS, but seemed like overkill, so to speak. When I'd asked if he lived here, he responded that he wasn't here often. I took it to be a vague affirmation. But why did he? And why would whoever owned the castle go to the trouble and expense to have such elaborate security measures installed?

Unless the owner was someone who also worked at SIS but at a higher level. Maybe his boss. Or his boss' boss. Then it would be more logically explained.

Once I had my laptop powered up, the first thing I'd do would be to search castles in the west of Scotland, then see if I could figure out who owned it.

Actually, it wouldn't be the first thing. I needed to attempt to get in touch with someone and let them know I was okay. Who, though? Clive? When I recalled the conversation I'd overheard, I thought better of it. Given the offices were closed for the holiday, no one would be expecting to see me anyway.

As far as anyone else realizing I was "missing," it wasn't as though I checked in with my parents daily or even weekly.

My mum would call occasionally, but given I'd spoken with her only a couple of days ago, it was unlikely I'd hear from her again before Christmas. Even then,

I'd told her I wouldn't be able to spend the holidays with them this year due to my workload. I doubted she'd bought it, but that our relationship was strained wasn't a secret to either of us.

The next thing I'd need to do would be to see if anything had hit the wires about what had happened at Edinburgh Castle last night.

"Apart from what was in your car, is there anything else you need?" Mrs. Drummond asked.

"A cup of tea would be nice."

"I'll get it," she said when we both walked toward the small kitchen. I watched her fill the electric kettle with water.

It was in my nature to ask questions both about the estate and the man who'd brought me here. However, grilling her would put her in an awkward position, given her employment.

I gazed out the window at the castle above, thinking about the body language I'd picked up on between David and Angus. Oddly, it was almost as if the man who'd saved my life was the other man's superior.

I glanced at Mrs. Drummond, who was studying me.

"Yes?" I asked.

"Nothing. Oh, there's David now."

"I'll get the door," I offered since she was pouring hot water into the cups.

"Thanks," he muttered. "Where would you like me to put this?"

The box was huge. "Uh, bedroom so it isn't in your way?"

I followed him down the hall, and he set it on the floor before turning and leaving. I shut the door behind him, anxious to find my laptop and mobile.

I caught his and Mrs. Drummond's muffled voices but couldn't make out anything they were saying. A few seconds later, I heard the front door close. When I peeked out of the bedroom window, I saw David walking away from the cottage and down the same trail I'd seen him on earlier.

"Bloody hell," I muttered when I saw the amount of rubbish that had been in my car and was now in the box. Had I really had all this garbage in there? It was a wonder it didn't smell. Or perhaps it had and I'd gone noseblind.

My computer was completely dead, of course, and I didn't see a charging cable in the box. Not that I kept one in my car that I recalled. The thing I didn't find that I was certain had been in it, was my mobile.

After sifting through and making sure all that was left was trash, I took the box back out to the main room.

"Is there a place where I can discard this?" I asked.

"I can take it for you," she offered.

"Much appreciated, but if you'll just point me in the direction of where to go, I'll handle it."

"If you set it outside, either David or Angus will take care of it."

"Yes, outside would be best," I said, chuckling.

When I opened the door and lowered the box to the ground, I saw David approaching. He was on his mobile, and while I couldn't hear what he was saying, he appeared angry.

"I'd ask if everything is okay, but one, I know it isn't, and two, you wouldn't answer me anyway."

"Apologies," he muttered.

My eyes widened.

"Oh, don't look so bloody surprised. I am capable of being sorry."

"Sorry. It's just that…"

"Go ahead. Out with it."

I shook my head. "I'd rather end the conversation with you saying something nice to me."

"Don't get used to it." He pointed to the box at my feet. "Rubbish?" he asked.

"Yes."

"*Good Lord*, what all was in your car?"

"*Stop.* Don't say another word. I'm going back inside and will pretend the last thing I heard was you apologizing."

Once there, I realized I hadn't mentioned my missing mobile. When I stepped out the door to do so, I looked in either direction he could've gone, but didn't see him.

6

Savior

I couldn't help but smile when Sullivan walked away. It was astonishing how similar she was to the girl I remembered. Not physically, of course, but in the way she said what she thought and could be relentless when she wanted to know something. Obviously, the mark of a good reporter. A profession I'd been guarded with most of my life, even before I was hired at SIS.

Knowing I wanted to go into intelligence meant, as the then-Marquess of Ravenscroft, I had to maintain a low profile. When my father passed away prematurely three years ago and I became the Duke of Ashcroft, it became doubly important that I keep my likeness out of the press as much as possible.

Con—more than even SIS—stayed on top of any potential sightings of me and had images and reports disappear moments after they went live. Not just for me but for himself, Tag, and Gus too.

Years ago, Con created what he called the Data Center, a place dedicated to safeguarding the privacy of his clients. It wasn't his only business. He also owned an ultra-elite private membership club, which provided high-adventure experiences to those who paid millions of pounds to join. Added to that was a whiskey distillery and a renewable-energy collaborative.

I didn't kid myself into thinking he'd given up some of his morally gray holdings. I kept my distance from them, and Con respected my desire to. The one I had made use of and planned to again today was a subsidiary of the Data Center dedicated to collecting information about anyone doing business in the United Kingdom.

Last night, after Sullivan retired to the bedroom, I'd sent him a message, asking that he dig up everything he could on Eric Weber and Tower-Meridian.

When he responded this morning, he suggested we meet, which raised the question of where.

I wasn't prepared to read Sullivan in on my true identity as the Duke of Ashcroft, the roles my closest friends played, or even for her to meet them. Which meant the obvious place for us to get together, other than the cottage, was the castle, made impossible by my uncle's arrival yesterday.

When I posed the question back to Con, he suggested Tag's place might be best. I was still mulling over whether that would work when Gus approached.

"How are you holding up?" he asked, squeezing my shoulder.

I smiled. "As much as I shouldn't be the one you're asking that of, I have to admit, I'm at odds with my own life presently."

Gus chuckled. "The lone wolf has no idea what to do with himself. Or better put, what to do with the woman currently under his protection."

He was right about me being a lone wolf. It had been months since I even saw him, Con, or Tag, and then it had been for the latter's father's funeral. I was rarely the first person to reach out to any of them, and when they contacted me, I typically took a long time to respond.

"Con said he wants to meet."

Gus nodded. "Have you heard from Typhon?"

I rolled my shoulders. "I have, and the news isn't good."

When he looked off in the distance, I knew he'd spoken to him as well.

"While she vehemently denies fabricating the order to take Sullivan out along with the gunman, the evidence is piling up against Periscope. I anticipate the nail in the coffin, so to speak, will come from Con."

"It already has," said Gus.

"Dammit," I muttered. "Why, though?"

"Con suggested we let her lead us to the answer."

My eyes widened. "How?"

"By allowing her to believe she's in the clear and is still your handler, but making the Weber investigation her main focus."

The plan made sense. "Right. Now, what are your thoughts on meeting at Tag's?" I asked.

"That's why I came to talk to you. Brose left a few minutes ago and said he wouldn't be returning until tomorrow or the next day."

I breathed a sigh of relief that he was gone. I just wished it wasn't temporary. "I don't understand why he insists on spending the holidays here. It isn't like we do anything."

As Gus knew, the only reason I visited around this time of year was to give my thanks, personally deliver bonuses, and give the staff that maintained the main residence and grounds them the rest of the season off to spend with their families. That alone made Brose's visits more curious. He typically expected to be waited on hand and foot but was left to fend for himself when the staff was on holiday themselves.

"By the way, I intend to inform your mother that this year is no different than any other as far as closing shop through the end of the year."

"Good luck with that," he said, shaking his head. "She'll not listen as long as there is a guest on the premises."

"Sullivan's hardly a guest," I muttered.

"I'll leave you to argue that point." He motioned toward the loch. "Do you have time for a walk?"

"Of course."

We took the trail to the far side of the island and stepped inside the cottage I hadn't visited in years prior to this morning.

"It's coming along," I commented, looking around the space that appeared to have been gutted on the inside. "You never said why you proposed this place be fixed up."

"It wasn't my idea. It was my mum's."

"Ah. Does she want to live in it, then?"

Gus shook his head. "I don't believe she does, and when I questioned her about why she made the request, she launched into a ten-minute monologue about how she's never asked for anything in all the years she's worked here."

"You know I'd never begrudge her anything, but don't you find it odd?" I asked.

"Very much so. Her second request is even more puzzling."

I raised a brow. "Go on."

"She asked that one room be left untouched—your grandfather's study."

He motioned me to the closed door, and when I opened it and stepped inside, I swore I could smell pipe tobacco. I hadn't set foot in here since I was sixteen, when he passed away, but I remembered this room being his sanctuary. He always said there was no place on the entire estate that had a better view of the loch— even from the castle.

Approaching the bookcases, I ran my hands along the spines, recalling I'd done the same as a child. "Look at this," I said, picking up a framed photo. "Is this you and me?" I asked.

Gus studied it with scrunched eyes. "I think it is."

"I've never noticed it before."

He shook his head. "Neither have I. In fact, I don't think I've ever seen a picture of the two of us."

I perused the rest of the room as though it was a time capsule. "My grandmother died before I was born," I said, picking up a photo of her from the desk.

"She was a beautiful woman," Gus said, looking over my shoulder. "As was your mum."

It was sad that both women died so young. Not just the two of them, but my father was only fifty when he passed—three years after my mother had.

"Out of your parents and grandparents, your paternal grandfather was the only one who lived beyond his fifties," Gus commented.

"Right," I said, returning the photo to the desk and noticing there wasn't a speck of dust anywhere on its surface. In fact, there wasn't any on the bookshelves either. It had been thirteen years since anyone had lived in the cottage. Surely, it hadn't been cleaned on a regular basis over the course of all those years.

"When we meet, Con can give us an idea of how long it will be before construction is complete, and then you can make a decision about where to stay," Gus added.

"Pardon? I didn't follow."

Gus had wandered out of the office. "You and Sullivan could stay here rather than in the smaller cottage."

He made a good point. However, based on the way it looked presently, it would be quite some time before it was inhabitable.

"Con and Tag are here," he said, looking at his mobile.

"Let them know we'll meet them in my office."

Gus nodded, knowing I spoke of the one I kept in the castle.

"Have you come to any decisions about revealing your title to Sullivan?" he asked on our walk back.

"The longer we're at Ashcroft, the more difficult it will be to keep it a secret. Especially with Brose's arrival." I stopped walking and put my hands on my hips. "This is *my* bloody home. Why is it I don't feel as though I can tell my uncle he isn't welcome to descend on the place as though it's his?"

Gus chuckled. "Only you can answer that question, Ash."

"We could always refurbish his suite of rooms. In fact, you could pull the crew from the cottage and have them start work this afternoon."

"We could do. And it would certainly be far easier than simply confronting him."

"Sod off," I muttered.

7

Savior

"Ash, great to see you," said Tag when Gus and I walked into the room where he and Con were waiting. I embraced both men, then invited them to take a seat.

"Interesting spot you've put yourself in," said Con.

I hung my head and shook it. "Not my doing, but my lot now, I suppose."

"Yes, but it's *Sullivan Rivers*." He tossed a dossier on the desk.

I chuckled and pointed at the document. "Please tell me that doesn't include the mad crush I had on her when we were children."

He smirked. "It didn't, but I added it."

"What have you got for me?" I asked.

"Before we talk about Eric Weber or Tower-Meridian, you should know the Crown Herald has had a massive data breach," said Con.

My eyes opened wide when the first thing I thought was what this might mean for Sullivan. "Are they aware?"

"They are now. I informed the newly named editor in chief, Fallon Wallace, as soon as I learned of it."

"I'm not going to ask what you charged them to fix it."

"Fallon and I are having dinner."

Both Tag and I laughed. "Is she buying? Somehow, I doubt the tab will cover it."

"I have bigger plans."

"As in they become a client?" I asked.

"There couldn't be a more fitting way to show her their vulnerabilities." He wove his fingers together and put his hands behind his head. "Sullivan's data was scoured."

"Gone?"

Con smirked again. "Only temporarily. By the way, from what little I saw, SIS would do well in convincing her to join the dark side."

I grimaced. "I consider the media the dark side, my friend."

"I concur," said Tag.

Con shrugged. "Either way, she's really good, Ash."

"Define good."

"According to Fallon, one of the best she's seen. Sullivan reports to Clive Edwards, the Edinburgh bureau chief and executive editor of investigations but also her uncle. I wouldn't be surprised if she were offered his position after his retirement. Maybe even before."

"If she's that good, Weber knows it. Which means the risk is even greater," I muttered.

"I can tell you that Weber's people are already looking for her," Con added.

"Why, though? I mean, what's she got on them?"

"Not enough, yet. However, that they are in pursuit tells me she's closer than even she realizes."

Tag stood and walked to the window.

"What's on your mind?" I asked him.

"If I were you, I'd bring her under the SIS umbrella as soon as possible," he said, glancing over his shoulder at me. "Of course, then, her bylines will go away."

I wasn't certain Sullivan would care. Somehow, I instinctively knew it was the investigation and its outcome that mattered more to her than the glory of being the one given credit for it. "What about Periscope?" I asked.

"Good point."

"I don't believe it will take long for her to hang herself," Con commented. "Then, talk to Typhon about Sullivan working under him."

"Unit 23 doesn't conduct investigations."

All three men raised their heads, but only Con spoke. "Since when?"

"Not official ones," I responded.

"Who suggested this would be official?" Tag said more than asked.

"Let's circle back to this later. Tell me about Eric Weber," I said to Con.

"I've not much yet. The man is shrouded in layers upon layers of mystery. As is Tower-Meridian. At least anything of substance. On the surface, they engage in global shipping and logistics. Given the resources the Crown Herald must've put behind Sullivan's investigation in terms of man hours alone, they must've discovered something."

"The most obvious would be human or weapons trafficking," said Tag.

"What could she possibly have on them that would be worth the risk of killing her?" My question was rhetorical, not that any of us would have an answer anyway.

"To be honest, I can't decide whether I'm glad I turned him down as a client five years ago or if it was the worst decision I ever made."

The unsavory part of Con's work was a sore spot for Tag, me, and Gus, who was being unusually quiet. We'd collectively agreed to a "don't ask, don't tell" policy before Tag and I joined Unit 23.

Had he signed Tower-Meridian, the moral dilemmas he faced would've been great indeed. It was a fine line he walked. One I wasn't cut out for.

Con shook his head. "I can tell you this much; whoever he did end up hiring has done a damn good job of keeping him well hidden."

"Are you actually admitting someone is as good as you are?" said Tag.

"I didn't say *as* good; I just said good."

Given Con was better than anyone else at SIS, he had every right to brag. I was once again reminded that

I'd have been outed years ago as the Duke of Ashcroft if it wasn't for him working his magic.

"What are you thinking, Gus?" I asked, drawing him into the conversation.

"If she's as good as her boss is saying and Con is concurring, then it might serve you better to come clean now rather than wait."

I leaned forward and rested my elbows on my knees. My gut was telling me it was too soon to reveal that Ashcroft was entailed to me. As much as I respected Gus' opinion, I had to follow my own instincts.

"Does Fallon know Sullivan is under SIS protection?" Tag asked.

"Negative. I plan to tell her tonight."

I raised a brow. "Tonight?"

"She's coming to Blackmoor." Con leaned forward like I was. "This is your call, Ash, but I think you should let Sullivan work while she's here."

"It *isn't* my call. I'm the glorified bodyguard."

All three men laughed, Gus harder than the other two.

"Admit to yourself this is personal," said Tag.

"Whether it is or not, I'm not in a position of deciding how much access to the outside world Sullivan has. As you're all well aware, it's for her protection."

"And you know bloody well that Con will be monitoring it as well as blocking anyone from finding her," Tag added.

"What are you suggesting? A delay in anything outgoing? If so, who will manage it?"

Gus raised his hand.

I looked between my three friends. "It's decided, then?"

"Not until it's unanimous," said Tag.

"I could see opening up online access but not mobile."

"Agreed," said Con. "Plus, from what I've seen, Miss Rivers might very well find a workaround that none of us pick up on. At least this way, we control it from the start."

"I need to think it over."

"Thistle Gate," said Gus, looking at his mobile.

"Pardon?"

"According to my mum, that's what your grandfather called the cottage."

I cocked my head. "I've never heard it referred to as such."

"The one you're in now was Primrose Croft."

"On that subject," said Con, pulling out a roll of plans. "Can we take a moment to review where that project stands?" He rested the stack on the desk and put paperweights on all four corners.

While I would've preferred we get straight to the discussion about Tower-Meridian, I nodded.

"The cottage's original exterior was stone on top of granite. My guess is when the castle was constructed, Thistle Gate was the next dwelling built." He looked over at me. "From a security standpoint, it works in our favor, Ash. Once we add bulletproof windows and doors, it will be nearly impenetrable. On the off chance someone figures out a way to get in, I've a suggestion." He rolled the top sheet to the left.

"Is that a panic room?" I asked.

He nodded. "Much smaller than what's beneath us."

"That's a dungeon, not a panic room," muttered Gus.

"Same difference," said Con. "Except for how to get in and out." He rolled the next sheet like he had the first.

I gasped. "What is *that*?"

"You'll never believe it. In fact, it makes me wonder about inbreeding between our two families."

"How so?" Not that it was the question I really wanted the answer to.

"Your ancestors were bloody brilliant, Ashcroft. Which means I must descend from them somehow."

I shook my head and chuckled. "Tell me what I'm looking at."

"There's a tunnel system between the island and the mainland," Con explained.

"It cannot be viable," I said.

He raised a brow and glanced over at Gus. "Tell him."

"It is."

"Tell him how you know."

Gus raised his middle finger. "Sod off, arsehole."

"Perhaps you can enlighten Ash another time," Con teased.

"You can't be serious. Were you in it?" I asked.

Gus shook his head. "Not me."

"Who, then?"

"Let's table this discussion for now," he muttered.

"Perhaps we should table it entirely," I added, sensing Gus' discomfort.

His expression turned serious. "I concur."

"Can we go back to the second drawing?"

Con unfurled it.

"Is this the last of the work to be completed on the cottage?" I asked.

He looked at Gus.

"Adding the necessary security to any refurbishment always takes place once the rest of the construction is finished and those crews are gone."

"Then, we're looking at seventy-two hours max," Con answered.

"That is equally remarkable and disappointing."

"How so?" he asked.

"His accommodations in the smaller cottage aren't exactly comfortable, given the sofas' length is half Ash's height," Gus responded.

Con chuckled. "Just sleep with her instead of on the sofa, Ash. You know it's going to happen eventually."

Like Gus had, I raised my finger and indicated the bastard should sod off.

"I told him he should simply banish Brose."

Con nodded. "I do have one other suggestion, though. It will make things far easier on everyone."

"Go on," I said.

"Relocate to Glenshadow until the security installation is complete."

"What's this?" Tag raised his head, given Glenshadow was the fifteenth-century monastery that had been converted into his family's home on the estate.

"That way, Ash can sleep in a bed and Sullivan won't be underfoot. The less she's about, the faster the crews can get the larger cottage ready to move into."

I glanced over at Gus. "There aren't tunnels between Primrose Croft and the castle, are there?"

"God forbid," he said under his breath.

There was a story there that Angus definitely didn't want to tell. Somehow, I suspected that if I pressed hard enough and got him to, I'd regret it. Lingering in the back of my mind was that whatever it was had something to do with his mother's request the cottage be refurbished.

"Throw your back out, confront your uncle, or relocate to the abbey. Those are your choices as I see them," Gus muttered.

Like we both had with Con, I raised my middle finger in his direction.

"See what fun we have in your absence?" Tag nudged me. "You should spend more time here."

"I don't think there's ever been a stronger case for staying away for longer periods of time."

"Is it settled, then? Temporary relocation to Glenshadow?" Con asked.

"As long as Tag is okay with it," I said at the same time my mobile vibrated. "What now?" I muttered, looking at the alert.

"Share with the class, Ash," Con teased.

"Mrs. Drummond relayed a message that Sullivan is requesting I return to the cottage"—I reread the message to be sure—"in the next fifteen minutes."

"What's this about?" Gus asked.

"It doesn't say." I looked over at Tag. "What are your thoughts on relocating her?"

"Of course. Whatever's necessary."

"Very well. See you later, gents." I stood and walked out.

No doubt all three men found my abrupt departure curious. Unless I was assigned an op, I was hardly known to jump when issued a demand. In fact, I'd be more likely to ignore it. Something told me Sullivan wouldn't play this card, though, if whatever it was, wasn't urgent.

8

Sullivan

I was stunned but happy to find a power cord for my laptop as well as ports built into the desk in the bedroom. While I waited for it to charge enough for me to use it, I returned to the living room and perused the books on the shelves.

Mrs. Drummond was still in the kitchen, tidying up even though it looked perfectly clean to me.

She'd been so gracious and kind to me thus far, I hesitated to pose the questions I was dying to ask. Surely, she would know the history of the castle and why security measures were so tight on an estate where an SIS sniper lived in a one-bedroom cottage.

For the second time, I talked myself out of it.

I glanced out the window, wondering where David had run off to in such haste.

Deciding it wouldn't be right for me to ask Mrs. Drummond about his whereabouts either, I leaned down to look at some of the larger books on the bottom section, elated when I saw one about Scottish castles.

I pulled it, along with a couple of others, from the shelves and carried it into the bedroom without glancing at Mrs. Drummond to determine whether she'd noticed or not.

As anxious as I was to see if the castle was in the book, I had far more urgent matters to attend to now that my computer was charged enough to power on.

I searched for a Wi-Fi network, stunned when I found one that didn't require a password. However, after pulling up the log-in page for the Crown Herald servers, the connection dropped.

Next, I tried an encrypted app I used to contact sources I didn't want the news agency I worked for to have access to. It had a built-in connection log, which immediately appeared on the screen.

```
Standard Wi-Fi: Blocked
Mobile data: Limited
Satellite connection: Intercepted
Secure VPN: Rerouted
```

While all this sounded standard, the intercepted satellite connection and rerouted VPN were mildly suspicious and majorly frustrating.

Irritated by my inability to access the outside world, I picked up the book about Scottish castles. After skimming the pages, I was disappointed not to find any photos that looked similar to the one that sat on the promontory above the cottage. I turned back to the copyright page and saw the publication date was four decades ago, not that much would've changed with structures that were centuries old.

I heard the front door open and close, and when I peeked out the window, I saw Mrs. Drummond walking down the trail in the direction of the loch. Odd that she hadn't knocked or called out that she was leaving. That she was gone, though, gave me the opportunity to do more exploring.

Something felt off about the place, almost as if it had been designed for a movie set. While everything in it looked authentic, it didn't feel that way.

Since I didn't have my mobile, something that still infuriated me, I made do with what I did have. I returned to the bedroom and grabbed my laptop. While using it to capture images wasn't ideal, it would suffice.

It took me a few minutes to get the camera angle right, but once I had, I raced around, collecting as many photos as I could. Periodically, I'd look out the window to be sure neither Mrs. Drummond nor David were in the vicinity.

I returned to the bookshelves, studying the titles more closely than I had earlier. Many were recent releases but in a multitude of genres with no set pattern. It was almost as though they were chosen as props rather than by someone interested in reading them. I was about to pull a crime-related hardback out when I glanced toward the window and saw Mrs. Drummond approaching. I quickly returned to the bedroom and set my computer on the desk. I was headed out to the living room and gasped when something occurred to me.

"Where's David?" I asked.

Mrs. Drummond looked up from where she was making another cup of tea. "Is there something you need, luv?"

"I must speak with him right away." I looked up at the clock on the wall. "Is that right?"

She glanced behind her, then at her watch. "It is."

I counted the number of hours I had left before the "dead man's switch" protocol I'd set up for my investigation would activate.

I'd already missed the first twelve-hour digital check-in. If I didn't do it before the twenty-four-hour mark, level-one activation would automatically commence.

First, the news agency would be notified of my disappearance. No doubt they'd stage a press conference. Then Clive would be alerted to where he could find my notes. It wouldn't be all of them. Those would come in increments, based on how much time had passed between check-ins. Theoretically, if I were dead, Clive would have all of it within a maximum of forty-eight hours. Given what I'd overheard of his conversation, I couldn't risk him accessing any of the investigation, even the preliminary notes.

"It's imperative I speak with him in the next fifteen minutes." I had more time than that, but who knew how long it would take before someone could arrange for me to have the access I needed.

"Of course," I watched as she pulled out her mobile and sent a message. The sight of it infuriated me all over again.

"Where the bloody hell is mine?" I muttered under my breath.

"Pardon?" she asked.

"My phone wasn't in the box with the other items," I snapped, immediately regretting my tone. None of this was Mrs. Drummond's fault.

"I hope it didn't get tossed with the rest of the rubbish," she said.

I'd sifted through it more than once before, deciding nothing else of import was in the box, so I was certain it hadn't been.

"Perhaps you should take another look."

While I doubted it would miraculously turn up in the stuff I'd unpacked and left scattered on the bed, it was at least worth a try. I was about to return to the bedroom, but when I glanced out the window and saw David approaching, I stepped outside instead.

There was something about the way he stalked toward the cottage that seemed familiar in the same way his eye twitch did. However, there was no way I'd met the man prior to his saving my life last night. If I had, I never would've forgotten him. Better put, my girly bits wouldn't have.

There was power in each step he took. It reverberated from every muscle in his chiseled body. The closer he got, the more I wanted to know how it felt to be in his arms with his mouth fused to mine. I slowly walked toward him.

"What's this about, Sullivan?" he asked when we were almost close enough to touch.

"Dead man's switch."

His eyes scrunched, then he nodded. "How much time do you have left?"

I wasn't surprised that he knew what I was referring to. "Approximately six hours before level-one activation. However, without a mobile or internet access, I have no way of checking in."

"Understood."

He pulled out his mobile. "Meet us at the cottage."

I looked beyond him a few seconds later and saw two men headed our way. "Who's that?"

"People I work with at SIS." He glanced over his shoulder, hesitated for a moment, then added, "They are also two of my closest friends. I trust them with my life. Therefore, I trust them with yours."

His response felt oddly *personal*. "David?"

He turned from looking at them to me. "Yes?"

"Have we met before?"

"Last night?"

Another curious response. "Yes, of course before last night."

"I don't know when it might have been."

I folded my arms and studied him when I saw the telltale eye twitch. We had met, but when? And why was he lying about it?

"I'll introduce you before we go inside," he said when they got closer.

"Um, okay."

"Sullivan Rivers, meet Conrad Carnegie and Niall MacTaggert, aka Con and Tag."

"It's a pleasure," said the one David pointed to first.

I shook his outstretched hand. "Likewise."

"Ms. Rivers," said the second one, bowing slightly, like Angus had when we met.

We walked over to the door of the cottage, and David waved me inside first.

"Give me a moment."

The two men and I stood a few paces inside while David spoke with Mrs. Drummond in hushed tones. The only thing I heard her say was, "Yes, of course, sir," before she gathered her things, waved in my direction, and walked out.

Now, I felt terrible for snapping at her as I had.

"Is she coming back?" I asked.

David studied me. "Is there something you need?"

"No, I just…Never mind."

After nodding once, closing the door, and locking it behind her, he motioned for us to take a seat.

"There are two issues with some urgency that need to be addressed," he began. "Con, I believe you can assist with the first. Tag, with the second." He turned to me. "Both men have been briefed by SIS as to why you are here. They're also aware of last evening's events at Edinburgh Castle and your investigation into Eric Weber and Tower-Meridian."

When both men nodded in my direction, David continued.

"As was prudent, either Ms. Rivers or the news agency she works for put a dead man's switch protocol in place in regard to the aforementioned investigation. The clock is ticking on the level-one activation."

Con pulled a computer out of a bag he brought in with him. "What are the digital check-in requirements?"

"All I need is internet access."

"While Con works on that, the other issue is relocation," said David.

My heart sank. He'd made it clear he didn't want to bring me here in the first place. More, he hadn't wanted to take on the burden of responsibility for me. He was a sniper, not a bodyguard.

"Where? Or is that information classified?"

I saw a hint of a smile. "An estate bordering this one."

I blinked away the threatening tears.

"Only temporarily," said Tag. "It's my estate, and I assure you, it's quite comfortable."

"While I appreciate it, I suppose the more important thing is that Eric Weber's associates are unable to find me." I thought about the hidden security here and that, even though I found it odd, it was reassuring.

While I hated to bring it up, I had to. "You said my mobile had to be destroyed to prevent tracking. Wouldn't the same be true for my laptop?"

"You're all set," said Con, looking up from his computer before David could respond. "What's this about Eric Weber and your laptop?"

"I assure you, the security systems at Glenshadow are state of the art," Tag interjected, then added, "Sullivan asked why her laptop hasn't been destroyed."

"It wasn't necessary to do so," said Con.

While I wanted to know why not, at this point, the conversation was disjunct enough I doubted anyone was even paying attention to me. Plus, I was more concerned about my eminent relocation. My gaze had alternated between David's two colleagues and him, but I couldn't read his expression. When his eyes met mine, then quickly looked away, I was crestfallen.

Good riddance, I supposed. After being here with him for less than twenty-four hours, it was silly to think I'd miss the man. Or he, me.

As much as I knew I should quit gawking, I couldn't. All three men were among the most handsome I'd ever seen.

Tag and Con looked as though they could be related. Both had dark hair and similar facial structures. Tag was clean-shaven, and Con had a scruffy beard, similar to David's, which was longer and ash-blond like his hair. It was unusual that each had different colored eyes. Con's were blue, Tag's brown, and David's green. Like so many things about him, they were familiar.

"So it's your estate that borders this one?" I asked Tag.

"Yes," he responded, glancing at David.

Something was at play here that I couldn't figure out. "How long have you known one another?"

"All our—"

"Careers," David interrupted Con.

The three also had similar speech patterns and accents. It was the former I found most curious, although if David grew up on the estate, I supposed he could've picked up the more affluent affectation.

"You should check in," David reminded me.

"Of course. Right. I'll do that now." I stood and went into the bedroom, stunned when he followed. I turned around and watched as he took in the mess left when I'd unpacked the box containing the contents of my car. "Sorry, I'll, uh, obviously, get this cleaned up, err, packed up." It occurred to me, then, I had nothing to put it all in. "I should've hung on to the box," I muttered.

"I'll have luggage sent round."

I'd tell him it wasn't necessary, but I had no other options.

He cleared his throat and pointed to my computer.

"Yes, right." I sat on the end of the bed and pulled up the Crown Herald's log-in screen. Unlike earlier, the connection was immediate, and I was successful in accessing the check-in protocol. "Done," I said, looking up at him. His gaze still swept the room. "Sorry, it's just that I emptied the box and…"

Why was I explaining myself? As soon as the luggage arrived, I'd clean everything up and be on my way. Perhaps I'd even ask if I could stay at Tag's place—Glenshadow, I thought he called it—for the duration of my "protective custody," so I wasn't underfoot here.

There was a knock at the door, and I bristled instinctively.

"That will be the bags," he said, turning to retreat down the hallway.

As much as I wanted to see what else I could access now that I had an online connection, it would be best if I packed my stuff quickly so I could leave. I moved my pile of things to one side of the bed so there'd be room to put the suitcase when David returned with it.

"Um, the clothes, should I—"

"Take them with you."

"Of course," I said under my breath, wishing such an innocuous answer didn't hurt as much as it did.

"We'll leave when you're ready."

"If you have other things to take care of, I'm sure Tag can—"

"I'll be staying at Glenshadow also."

"Oh. Uh, is that necessary?"

"Yes," he said before he abruptly turned and left.

Well, then, I thought, shaking my head and foolishly smiling.

9

Savior

I'd lied to Sullivan—many times, actually—but this time, it was about the necessity of me staying at Glenshadow with her. I didn't doubt Tag's ability to keep her safe, but the idea of not being able to see her bothered me far more than it should.

Based on the looks on my friends' faces, they'd heard our conversation.

"Shut it," I said before either of them spoke. I turned to Tag. "I appreciate this, mate."

"I'm beginning to regret not asking the lovely Miss Sullivan to stay with me," Con said barely above a whisper.

I glared at him, and he laughed.

"Let me help you with that," said Tag, looking over my shoulder, then brushing past me in the hallway.

"I've got it," I said too late.

"Thanks," Sullivan said, her eyes meeting mine since Tag's back was to her.

"Always," I said under my breath. Had we been alone, had she remembered me, had any number of circumstances been different, I would take her in my arms and promise that whatever she needed, whatever she wanted, I'd do everything I could to make it happen.

"Let's be off, shall we?" said Con, motioning to the door.

The drive from Ashcroft to Glenshadow was quick, but I didn't miss the way Sullivan took in her surroundings.

"It's so beautiful," she said once we were inside the estate's gates.

"Tag raises Highland cattle," I mentioned as we drove past two that were near the fence lining the road.

"They're adorable. I love coos." Her voice was wistful, even childlike, much as I remembered it being.

Maybe whichever of my friends had suggested I come clean with Sullivan about knowing her when we were children was right. Except now that I'd lied about not recalling meeting her previously, I'd have to own up to it. I tapped her arm and pointed to my side of the vehicle.

"Oh!" She gasped. "A baby coo. They're even sweeter." Her smile took my breath away, making me want to reach over and touch her hand with mine. I knew I should look away before she caught me staring, but I couldn't.

Her wide-eyed innocence at times like these belied the dogged determination that played out on her face with her endless stream of questions. I closed my eyes, imagining how her expression would change when I pulled her into my arms and kissed her for the first time.

"David?" she whispered.

There was no way for me to mask my desire with someone as perceptive as Sullivan. Instead, I eased my hand closer to hers and brushed her finger with mine.

I pulled away when Tag parked near the entrance to Glenshadow. "We're here."

Sullivan looked surprised when she raised her head. "That was quick."

"As Tag said, his land borders mine, err, you know, where I live." I couldn't look at her to see if she'd noticed the slip. It would only make her more suspicious.

I got out and went around to get her door.

"It's lovely."

"Perhaps after you're settled, Ash, err, David can show you around the place," said Tag.

While Sullivan appeared lost in thought, I doubted she'd missed this slip. It was the second in under a minute. How could three trained SIS agents, two of whom were assassins, no less, make such blunders? It was unfathomable.

"David? A moment?" said Con when Tag invited us inside.

"Go on. I'll catch up," I said, watching them walk away.

"You need to tell Sullivan you're the Duke of Ashcroft. Her situation is precarious at best, and her intuition is razor-sharp. She's already started to doubt if she can trust you, and it's for all the wrong reasons."

I respected Con's opinion above most others. Some of his personal dealings bordered on nefarious, but as far as being a true friend, there were few better.

"I will."

"When?" he pressed.

"Soon. I can't say precisely."

He smirked. "The longer you wait, the more diffi-cult it will be. Now, on to another subject. Have you heard anything more from Typhon?"

"Only that you all suspect Periscope, and honestly, it's the only thing that makes sense. Troubling as it is."

"Have the two of you ever…?"

I looked at him with wide eyes. "You can't be serious."

"I've taken a deeper look."

Based on his tone, he'd found something concerning enough to warrant this conversation. "And?" I asked, following him when he walked farther away from where Tag had parked.

"She's too efficient. Never a misstep."

"Gus mentioned your recommendation that she be misled into thinking she's in the clear."

He nodded. "Precisely. The idea is to keep her on as your handler, albeit without any pending assignments. Instead, make the Weber investigation her focus."

"As he also said."

"I've already set tracking up."

"Upon whose authority?"

Con looked away, which wasn't like him.

"Whose?" I repeated.

"Both Viper's and Typhon's."

"Without consulting me? Dammit, Blackmoor."

"As a reminder, I do not work for you, *Ashcroft*." It was typically only in anger that the three of us made use of our titles as lords.

"Considering I am responsible for Sullivan's protection in this instance, I would be first in your chain of command."

He raised a brow but didn't challenge my statement even though it was inaccurate. The way he'd handled it *was* according to protocol.

"Apologies," I muttered.

"Accepted. This isn't to usurp your authority, Ash. It's about monitoring Periscope, who has raised concern for all of us."

"You're right."

"Look. I'll say again that the best course of action is for you to be honest with Sullivan. Not only for her sake, but for yours too. You're wound tighter than I've ever seen, Ash."

He wasn't wrong, but before I could say anything else, we heard the door open and saw Tag approach. He appeared agitated in contrast to his usual unflappable demeanor, making my anxiety increase.

"What's happened?" I asked.

He handed me his mobile. On the screen was an alert about a tracking device, something his security picked up and mine had not.

"Let me see that," said Con, grabbing the phone from my hand. "This is one of mine." He looked between Tag and me.

"My first question is, was it intentional?" Tag asked.

"Of course it wasn't," Con responded in a raised voice. "If it had been, it would've been by consensus."

"What are you thinking?" I asked when he continued studying the screen.

"The only person who makes any sense whatsoever—again—is Periscope. She could've placed it with Sullivan's things after you took her from the parking lot."

I concurred and said so. "But how did she get her hands on one of your devices?"

"Damned good question, and one I intend to get answers to. I'll meet up with the two of you later," he said when Gus pulled up behind Tag's SUV. "Perfect timing," he muttered, getting in the passenger side and motioning for our friend to turn around.

"I've put the two of you in the east wing, and Sullivan is set up on the network," said Tag once they'd driven away.

"Which Con and Gus will monitor?"

"Affirmative."

"Were you aware Con is tracking Periscope?" I asked.

"I was not. However, I'm not surprised, and based on this"—he held up the mobile Con had returned to him—"its implementation is timely."

"Too timely?" I wondered out loud, hating that my instincts were questioning a man who was like a brother to me. "What's he up to, Tag?"

He looked off in the distance. "I wish I knew."

Once we were inside, I excused myself to the east wing and went in search of Sullivan. On the way to our rooms, I noticed her in the library.

"How goes it?" I asked when she raised her head.

"Not much new with Tower-Meridian. I feel as though I've been away from the investigation for days rather than hours."

"Perhaps I can be of assistance." My suggestion was to gauge whether Con was right about Sullivan's lack of trust in me. She hesitated, which I'd anticipated.

"How much do you know about Eric Weber?" she asked.

"Admittedly, not much outside of his public persona."

"Enlighten me."

I grinned. She was testing me, and rightly so. "He runs a global shipping and logistics company, which is well known for its philanthropic endeavors."

"Such as?" she prompted.

"Humanitarian aid and medical supply distribution as well as emergency response services and refugee support. They're also big in agricultural equipment and infrastructure development."

"All of what you've said is true, at least according to their well-publicized mission statement." It was several seconds before she spoke again. No doubt she was carefully weighing what she could or would divulge. Finally, she took a deep breath and let it out slowly as her eyes met mine. "Let me give you some insight as to how everything you mentioned provides a plethora of smokescreens to hide what he's really up to."

I was fascinated. "Go on."

She reached into her computer bag, rummaged around in it, and extracted a notebook that looked as though it had gone through the wash and dry cycles of a laundry machine. I studied her as she flipped through the pages, each of which were full of scribbled notes.

"Let's start with medical supplies…"

According to her research—and well-placed sources, I suspected—Sullivan had noted manifests showing full containers of the aforementioned supplies. She turned her laptop so I could see the two documents she'd pulled up on the screen.

"The arrival weights are significantly different from those taken at departure. This is also true of shipments containing humanitarian aid in the way of food supplies. Those were off by as much as thirty percent. Not to mention 'lost' containers and suspicious detours. At first, I just thought they were selling both on the black market."

"But then?"

"Temperature logs for sensitive medications were incomplete, inventory reports on the manifests don't match, there's so much missing documentation, and then this." She replaced the images on the screen with others.

I studied what appeared as much to figure out what they meant as to determine where they'd come from. Sullivan had sources in very high places.

"I won't divulge where I got this."

I looked from the screen to her. "I would expect not. Based on this alone, Tower-Meridian experienced not just communications blackouts but managed to block satellite tracking. At least on this particular shipment."

Sullivan shook her head. "All the manifests I've looked at are the same."

Something else occurred to me. "Can you go back to the previous one?" When she did, I leaned in for a closer look. "This vessel's home port is Tees." Most larger shipping companies in the UK were registered in Felixstowe, the largest port, by far.

"I could do an extensive exposé on corruption out of Tees alone."

I rested against the chair and looked at Sullivan rather than at her computer. "What's your theory?"

"At first, I was convinced Weber's primary business was trafficking in humans."

"Now?"

"Weber's patterns suggest sophisticated coordina-tion between Tees and Felixstowe. They appear to be exploiting the chaos inherent from traveling between two such different ports. Not to mention, the manifests are signed off on at the smaller of the two and spot-checked at the larger. Which, without the blackouts and dead spots, removes all suspicion."

There was something I was missing. "Your hypothesis is that they're loading weapons in Tees, then traveling to Felixstowe to pick up the aid-related supplies."

Sullivan shook her head.

"What, then?"

"There are no aid-related supplies."

"Meaning it's all designed as camouflage?" How in the bloody hell would that work? Even the most simplistic of manual checks would detect metal. "A single, well-timed raid would put them out of business and land Weber in prison for the rest of his life." I rested my crossed arms on the table. Someone like Con could've pieced this together in a fraction of the time it had taken Sullivan. Which meant he had done. The question now was, when? In the last few hours, or had he known far longer? I rolled my shoulders, knowing that sometime very soon, I'd be forced to have one of the hardest conversations of my life with a man who'd been my friend for the entirety of it.

"Have you been to your room?" she asked.

"I was on my way when I noticed you in here."

"Tag said mine wasn't ready yet, but it should be by now."

"Shall we go up together?" I asked as I watched her cram everything that sat on the table into her bag. "Perhaps a work area can be set up for the duration of our stay here."

She hesitated. While she'd trusted me enough to share her theories with me, it wasn't enough for her to leave her research unattended.

"We should talk," I blurted right before one of Tag's staff members walked past the library. "Privately."

10

Sullivan

The walk from the library to our upstairs rooms seemed endless. I was so anxious about whatever David intended to tell me. I just prayed he was ready to be truthful about the things I sensed he was either hiding or lying to me about.

I'd put a great deal of trust in him when I shared my theories about Eric Weber and Tower-Meridian, because deep down, even in the short amount of time we'd been together, I sensed I could. I just wished he felt the same way about me.

If confiding in him had been a mistake, I doubted I'd ever forgive myself for it. Then again, if I was really wrong, I might not live long enough for it to matter.

"This is me," I said when we reached the fourth door on the left, as Tag had written down for me. "Would you like to come in?"

"Um, sure. I think I'm just one over from you."

When we went inside, I saw we'd been given adjoining suites, the connecting doors of which had been left open.

"Do you know what this is?" David asked, chuckling.

"Besides adjoining suites?"

He motioned for me to join him in the other room.

"When Tag's ancestors first converted the monastery into their home—and we're talking a couple of centuries ago—this would have been the earl's quarters." He pointed to my suite. "And those would belong to the countess."

"Of course. I see that now. Seems so unromantic."

"While I'd venture to guess some unions may have been based on love, the majority were arranged and were more of a business deal than a marriage."

"What about your family, David?"

His eyes met mine. "Sullivan…I…"

An alert that sounded like an alarm went off on his mobile.

"Come with me," he said, taking my hand in one of his and pulling me from the room.

"What's going on?" I asked when I realized he'd drawn his gun with the other.

He grasped my hand tighter. "This way," he said when the power went out and the only illumination was from the lights along the floorboards.

"Is there a fire?"

"Something like that." He pulled me into a room at the end of the hallway. "Stay as close as you can to me."

He used his shoulder to push against a panel in the wall and, when it opened, led me behind it. The temperature immediately dropped by several degrees.

"The steps are steep," he warned. "Hold onto my arm and stay as close as you can behind me."

"David, please tell me what's happening," I whispered.

"Security breach. There's a safe room on the lowest level, and that's where I'm taking you."

I hugged the stone wall as we made our way down what felt like two stories. Unlike in the hallway, there was no illumination in the musty-smelling stairwell. Once we got to the bottom, David reached into his pocket. Seconds later, the place where we stood was lit up by his mobile.

When he pointed it at a door, I saw a panel similar to the one outside his cottage entrance. He placed his palm on it, and another smaller door sprung open. There, he punched in a code. "Con seriously needs to rethink this," he muttered, leading me through the now-unlocked entrance. "Although this is nicer than I imagined," he commented when motion-detected lights turned on and the door shut and locked behind us.

My mouth gaped, less at the room we were in than at his surprisingly nonchalant attitude.

"Come here," he said, pulling me close to him.

"David, this is…"

"Shh," he soothed, stroking my hair when I couldn't speak and my body began to shake.

My eyes flooded with tears, something that was rare for me.

"Come and sit."

I let him lead me to a sofa and pull me down beside him. "I have a few things to tell you."

"A few?" I said in a raised voice.

"Yes. Well, a couple, at least."

I wriggled my hand from between his. "I was thinking it was a higher number."

"I'm not sure where to start."

"How about with who you really are?"

He turned his body to face me and reached for my hand. "Please," he said when I moved it out of his grasp.

His eyes bored into mine. "My name is David Evans." He paused as though he expected it to mean something to me. When my eyes scrunched and I shook my head, he continued.

"What I told you about who I work for was the truth—"

"You didn't tell me. You said that a decent reporter would be able to figure it out. Maybe not those exact words, but close."

"Sounds like me," he muttered. "I work for SIS, and as I'm sure you gathered, I am an assassin."

My eyes opened wide, and I gasped. "An assassin?"

"Yes, but I am on the side of the good guys." He added something under his breath that I didn't catch, but I also didn't ask him to repeat it.

"What else?"

"I am, as I'm sure you've guessed, the Duke of Ashcroft."

"The duke?"

"That's right. Given my, err, line of work, it's been necessary that I maintain a certain anonymity."

"You're a duke."

"Yes. Of Ashcroft—the castle and estate of the same name."

"So, why…?" My mind raced, answering my own question.

"There's more."

I nodded and averted my gaze. "Of course there is."

"A few years ago—actually longer than that—over twenty years ago, my family spent a year living in Ballater, outside—"

"I know where Ballater is. I grew up…" *Twenty years ago?* His family spent a year there? "My God. You're…"

"From what I remember, and that's everything from that year of my life, you called me Davy."

"Davy?" The name was barely a whisper on my lips.

"Yes, Sully."

My eyes darted between his until I finally squeezed them shut.

"I'm sorry I didn't tell you."

I jerked my hand from his. "I asked you repeatedly. I knew you were familiar." I raised my gaze and studied him. "You lied. Over and over again."

"I apologize, Sullivan. Sincerely."

Rather than ask, I thought about why he had. As much as it angered me, could I really fault him for it? Especially about being a duke. If I were in his place, I would've kept it a secret too. As far as him denying the familiarity, I was irritated that he hadn't just come out with it, but again, could I blame him?

"I didn't recognize you."

"I hardly hoped you would." He winked.

"You do look different." My voice trailed off as I recalled the little boy he used to be. "Wait, you recognized me?"

"Sullivan Rivers is a far more memorable name."

I nodded. "It is. *Far* more than just David."

"Yes, well."

I folded my arms in front of me. "Yes, well," I mimicked, taking a deep breath and looking around the room. "This is the craziest thing that's ever happened to me. Wait. Not the craziest. Having a gun against my head and thinking I was a split second away from dying is worse than this. But still."

"Can I ask which part?" It was such a relief to be able to place the look on his face. At that moment, he became Davy, the shy, sweet boy who my mum teased me about incessantly.

"I'm not sure." I looked around the room. "This, mainly. How much danger are we in?"

"I don't know except to say no one can get to you in here. The other thing is, it could very well be a false alarm, and by that, I mean someone could be trespassing on the estate, but their reasons for doing so have nothing to do with you being here."

"Such as?"

He stroked his beard, something I hadn't seen him do. "I'd say hunters, but we're quite far out of the season, aren't we?"

I stared at him. "Why are you so calm?"

"Calm? I'm not. I suppose what I am is not worried. We are in the safest place possible, perhaps in all of Scotland. With the exception of Con's estate, although I haven't had occasion to be in his safe room."

"You're also chatty."

His brow furrowed. *"Chatty?"*

"You've been quite tight-lipped."

"Yes, well, when keeping up a fabrication to conceal my identity, it's typically best to say as little as possible."

I turned and rested against the sofa. Flopped would be a better way to describe it. "I should be really angry with you. More, I should be questioning everything you're telling me. Maybe I should be afraid for my life."

"Are you?" he asked.

"What?"

"Doing anything of those things?"

I shook my head. "Stupidly, not. Or maybe it's sadly."

"I'm glad."

"Argh," I groaned when my eyes filled with tears.

David put his arm around me and pulled me close to him, stroking my hair like he had a few minutes ago.

"I won't hurt you, Sullivan. I won't let anyone else hurt you, either."

"I know," I whispered, brushing at my tears.

"Why are you crying?"

His question only made it worse. How could I admit that I had so few people in my life who I could trust, so few people I even confided in, that here I was, believing him. A man who'd lied to me repeatedly, could've killed me, and who I hadn't seen in over twenty years.

A man who, in reality, was a complete stranger to me, and yet, I felt safe and protected. When he said he wouldn't let anyone hurt me, I believed him. God, I *trusted* him. "I don't even know you," were the only words I managed to say.

His hand moved to my cheek, and he raised my face. "Don't you, Sullivan? Or do you know me better than anyone?"

His lips were soft against mine. Sweet, gentle, and loving. Not at all what I wanted. I angled my head, pressed my tongue against his mouth, and when he opened to me, I deepened the kiss and wrapped my arms around his neck. He pulled me onto his lap, then put one hand on the back of my neck and the other around me, cupping my bottom.

I froze when I heard someone outside the door, breaking the kiss, but closing any space there was between our bodies.

"All clear," I heard Tag shout right before the door sprung open. He took one look at us, arms entwined, bodies flush, then backed his way out of the room.

"Right. As I said, all clear. Take your time." The sound of his voice grew more distant with each word he spoke.

I rested my head against David's chest. "I'm mortified."

He put his fingers on my chin and raised my face. "I'm not, and what's more, Tag isn't, either."

"No?"

He shook his head. "In fact, he, Con, and Gus, if they're here, are likely drinking a toast to us right now."

"Should we join them?"

David shook his head. "Not just yet. I've twenty years of wanting to kiss you to make up for."

11

Savior

I held Sullivan's hand as we made our way up the same narrow staircase we'd come down, but instead of going up to the second floor, I stopped at the first.

Con, Tag, and Gus were waiting for us in the library. Based on their expressions, the breach wasn't as innocuous as I'd hoped.

"What do we know?" I asked, deciding straightaway not to hide anything from Sullivan unless it was absolutely necessary I do so.

Con's eyes met mine, and I nodded once.

"There were three armed intruders, and accessing the property was not accidental," he said.

Sullivan was standing beside me, and her hand brushed mine. I took it like I had when we walked up the stairs, then led her to a chair.

"Was it Weber?" she asked.

"We haven't yet been able to make that determination. However, it's a logical theory."

"Are they in custody?" I asked.

"Negative," Tag responded.

"What did you learn about the tracking device?" I asked Con.

"I've confirmed it was one of mine."

There were several things I needed to discuss with Con, but none that I would with an audience. Deciding it was best to delay until the following day, I suggested we reconvene in the morning unless there were additional pressing issues to be addressed.

"What about relocating?" I asked.

"Not until we've had the chance to reevaluate the systems at Ashcroft," said Gus.

My eyes met Sullivan's. "You should all be aware that I've briefed Ms. Rivers on my true identity as it relates to my estate. I've also filled her in on our shared past."

None of my three friends appeared surprised.

"Good," said Con.

I glanced over at Sullivan, who hadn't spoken. No doubt she was in shock, more from the breach and visit to the safe room than the truths I'd revealed. Still, she and I needed time alone.

"Is there anything else we need to discuss presently?" I asked.

None of the three men in the room spoke up.

"In that case, Sullivan and I will excuse ourselves."

She looked up at me and stood when I held my hand out to her.

"Shall I arrange for dinner to be brought up?" Tag asked.

"That would be lovely. Many thanks," I said.

Our walk upstairs was done in silence.

"You're very quiet," I said once we reached the first of the two suites.

"Processing. Would you like to come in?"

"Very much so, unless you'd prefer to be alone."

She wrapped her arms around her waist. "That's the last thing I want to be."

I walked over to the fireplace. "Cold?"

"A bit."

As I lit the logs Tag or someone else had laid, I thought about how, while we were in the safe room, I'd felt like I had so much to say, so much I wanted to tell Sullivan, and now, I struggled for words.

As I watched the kindling catch, I also thought about the heat of the kiss we'd shared. If only it could've lasted longer. If only we could do it again.

"What are you thinking about?" she asked from behind me.

"Kissing you." I glanced over my shoulder and winked.

"Truly?"

I stood and joined her on the two-seater sofa. "What about you?"

When I put my arm across the back of the cushions, Sullivan rested her head on my shoulder. "I remember you."

"Yeah?"

"I think you might have been my first crush."

I'd not say it, but even now, when I thought back on it, it felt so much bigger, so much more important than that.

"Things my mum said make more sense to me now."

"What things?" I asked.

"Apparently, even at eight years old, you were a catch."

I chuckled. "I have photos that would prove otherwise."

"She must've known your parents, err, owned a castle."

"We were living in Ballater because my father had work at Balmoral."

"Makes sense. I don't remember much about him, but I do recall your mother was beautiful."

I rested my cheek against her head. "She was."

"It's sad she passed so young."

"She and my father. Earlier today, Gus reminded me that my grandfather on my dad's side is the only one of the four who lived much beyond fifty."

"What about your mother's parents?" she asked.

"Sadly, there was an estrangement I never knew much about."

"Are they still living?"

"I'm not entirely certain," I admitted. "What about your parents?"

"My mum and dad are still with us. I don't see them often. She can be quite, err, overbearing." She shifted so I could see her face. "You used to pull my hair."

I smiled. "My apologies for doing so."

"This is awkward, right?"

I tightened my arm around her shoulders and squeezed. At first, I thought I'd make light of it. How could it not be? It hadn't been twenty-four hours since I'd whisked her out of a parking lot where, if

I'd followed the orders relayed to me by my handler, she would've breathed her last breath. What if it hadn't been me who was called to assist MI6? What if it had been Tag? Or another of Unit 23's assassins? I shuddered, thinking about what may have happened.

"I knew it was you last night," I confessed. "What I mean is, even if I hadn't been told your name, I still would've known."

"I suppose I should be very grateful you did." Her eyes scrunched. "That didn't come out the way I meant it. I *am* grateful. I must be honest; I'm also terrified."

The conversation we'd had earlier today about Eric Weber in itself was troubling, at best. There was still the question of why a man with the kind of power he appeared to have would want a reporter at Sullivan's level dead. Unless she either had far more on him than she was willing to admit or she hadn't yet figured out the significance of the things she'd unearthed in the course of her investigation.

It reminded me of the conversation I'd soon have to have with Con. And then I recalled he was meeting with Fallon Wallace this evening about the Crown Herald's data breach.

"I hesitate to change the tone of our conversation."

"Don't."

I studied her.

"I'm serious, David. I already feel as though I've lost five years of my life during the last twenty-four hours alone. Just for tonight, can we focus on happier times? Those when we didn't have a care in the world?"

"We can do."

"Did Tag say something about dinner? I'm suddenly starving."

"What do you say we take matters into our own hands?"

"Do you know where the kitchen is? I mean, castles have kitchens, right? I've not been in one where anyone actually resides in it any longer."

"Never tell Mrs. Drummond I said so, but not only is Tag's kitchen nicer than Ashcroft's, but his cook's food is better too."

"You never should've told me that, David." It occurred to me I'd never heard anyone address him that way.

"Why shouldn't I have told you about Tag's cook?"

"Blackmail, obviously, in an effort to get you to divulge more of your secrets."

I put my hand on Sullivan's cheek. "All you ever have to do is ask."

She chuckled. "If that's the case…"

"Yeah? Have you started a list?"

"Not yet, but I do have one question. How do people address you?"

"People?"

"Con, Tag, and Gus, mainly."

"Ash. Our bunch prefers single syllables, or so it seems. What about you? Do your mates call you Sully?"

She shook her head. "I don't really have many. Well, any mates to speak of. The people I work with refer to me as Bully."

"Bully? Why ever would they call you that?"

"I'm sure they meant it to be disparaging, but I took being likened to a bulldog as a compliment."

"Word is you're an exceptional investigator. That, I could've gathered based on your inquisitions alone."

Sullivan wiggled her finger in my direction. "Except we're not talking about work or anything related to it."

"As you wish, Sully."

After a delicious dinner of cullen skink—the traditional Scottish soup made from smoked haddock, onions, and potatoes—and crusty bread fresh from the ovens, Sullivan and I returned to our suites. As much as I wanted to stay and talk to her until the wee hours of the morning, I'd gotten very little sleep the night before. I'd noticed her yawn several times throughout our meal, so she was likely equally exhausted.

Rather than following her inside, I remained in the hallway. "Will you be able to sleep okay?" I asked. "Or shall I take you for a ride around the estate?" That got a smile out of her.

"Do you want to…?" She motioned behind her with her head.

"I think it best I don't tonight."

"Sure. Right. Of course."

"I would like to kiss you once more if you wouldn't mind."

"Not at all. We've twenty years to make up for, right?"

When I leaned forward, our lips met. The kiss was over far too soon, but if I didn't go to my rooms now, I might never.

"Good night, Sully."

"Good night, Ash. Or should I call you Davy?"

I smiled, shook my head, and walked the rest of the way down the hallway, happy to have a bed to sleep in tonight, but not quite as pleased that the opposite side would be empty.

After a quick shower, I got under the covers, but rather than sleep, I stared at the ceiling. We'd managed to remain cocooned in happy thoughts for the last couple of hours. Tomorrow morning, we'd have no such luxury. Me, especially.

When I woke with the sunrise, it was because my mobile pinged with an alert from Gus.

Periscope is ready to talk. She said only to you.

"Bloody hell," I muttered out loud. Doing so meant returning to Edinburgh, something I definitely didn't want to do, especially today.

I'd tossed and turned a good share of the night, making mental lists of action items for today, including a full briefing from Sullivan on her investigation, if she was willing. If so, I'd wait until after it was over to speak with Con privately. If she wasn't willing, I'd get it over with first.

Since I knew he was awake, I rang Gus rather than reply. "Can't Periscope speak with anyone else?" I said even before good morning, since it wasn't.

"It's you or no one, or so I've been told."

The woman was my handler; we weren't mates, for God's sake. I'd never been her confidant. In fact, we'd hardly spoken. "Why?"

Gus sighed. "While I can't be certain, I think it's because she knows Sullivan is with you. Or she strongly suspects it."

"And?"

"Someone got her to relay a fake kill order, Ash. Whoever it was still wants Ms. Rivers dead. To be honest with you, I found the notion of letting Periscope believe no one was on to her ridiculous."

"I agree. I was skeptical it would work."

"If the ultimate goal was to get her to confess her involvement with Weber and Tower-Meridian, you meeting with her is the quickest way to it."

"Right. On the subject of someone wanting Ms. Rivers dead, have you gotten anywhere with yesterday's intruders?"

"Making progress. They're definitely professionals. However, so are we."

"Where was the access point?" I asked, getting out of bed and pacing the room.

"We're still trying to piece that together."

I thought about some of the satellite images Sullivan had showed me yesterday. I knew where she'd gotten them, just not how. And after she'd specifically stated she wouldn't tell me, I wasn't sure how to broach it today.

"I'd like to have a team meeting this morning, which means if I have to give in to Periscope's demands, I won't be able to meet with her until this afternoon."

"Roger that. Let me see what I can do."

"Before you ring off. How's the security update going at Ashcroft?"

"Nearly done. In fact, Con's been here most of the night."

At any other time in my life, that would've filled me with confidence. Right now, what I felt bordered more on dread.

"What's going on, Ash?"

"I'll fill you in later. What time can the two of you be here?"

"Zero nine hundred."

"See you then. Oh, and did Con say whether he met with Ms. Wallace?"

"He did."

"And?"

"He said he'll fill us in later."

I thought about checking on Sullivan, but it seemed like a bit of an invasion of privacy. Plus, if I peeked into the room and saw her still in bed, the lure of joining her would be hard to resist.

Instead, when I came downstairs, I found her in the dining room, speaking with Tag.

"Good morning," I said, catching them both off guard. What precisely had they been discussing that resulted in my startling them in such a way?

"Ash," said Tag, getting up from his seat.

"Good morning," said Sullivan, looking over at me.

All I could think to ask was what was going on here, so I remained quiet, looking instead for tea. When I saw it and a modest breakfast set out on the sideboard behind me, I turned my back to both.

"Gus informed me Periscope is ready to talk but only to me."

"What will you do?" Tag asked.

"I've not much choice, do I?"

Without facing him, I knew he'd bristled. Maybe not visibly to Sullivan.

"Have you heard from Con this morning?" I asked before remembering Gus had said he was at Ashcroft.

"I anticipate he'll be here within the hour. I was just telling Sullivan I was anxious to hear about his meeting with Fallon Wallace."

When I turned around, my gaze met Sullivan's. Had she realized I'd kept the meeting from her?

"Prior to that briefing, I'll be meeting with him privately."

Tag nodded and retook his seat. Unlike what I would've expected from the usually inquisitive Sullivan, she didn't ask why.

When I sat at the table and noticed she had her laptop with her, I wished I would've thought to bring mine. Not that it would distract me enough to pull me out of my dark mood.

There was a reason I was a loner. I preferred silence over a conversation more often than not. Yes, kissing Sullivan had been a dream come true, but that was all it had been. A silly kid's fantasy come to life. After not seeing each other for over twenty years, we weren't friends. I wasn't certain if we had been even then.

"Are you all right?" Sullivan leaned in and whispered.

"Perfectly fine," I said right before taking a bite of the croissant I'd taken from the sideboard's breakfast offerings.

Before I finished eating, Gus and Con arrived. I was about to propose the private meeting I'd wanted with the latter, but thought better of it. As I reminded myself, my plan was for Sullivan to brief the crew, as Typhon called us, and study his reaction.

After suggesting we remain in the dining room, I excused myself to get my computer. I took the stairs two at a time, and when I came out of the suite after retrieving it, Sullivan was waiting for me.

"You seem angry."

"Professional. Not angry."

She folded her arms, and her head snapped back as if I'd struck her. Or threatened to. She spun on her heel and went downstairs.

"Sullivan—" When she didn't stop or respond, I returned to the suite and sat on the bed. A few minutes later, I heard a rap at the door.

My first reaction was to tell whoever it was to go away. On the off chance it was her returning, I got up and went to the door.

"Gus," I said, turning around.

"Ash. We're waiting on you."

"One would think you'd be able to conduct a meeting without my input."

"The meeting you called?"

"I didn't…I suppose I did."

He stepped inside and shut the door behind him. "Is this about Periscope?"

"In part. The other thing is I'm in unfamiliar territory with Sullivan. I handled things poorly yesterday. As a result, she's expecting her boyfriend to show up rather than a Unit-23 assassin who, at the end of the day, shouldn't be involved in her investigation. More, Typhon never should've assigned me detail work."

"Easy enough solution, then."

"What's that?"

"I'll contact Typhon and let him know I'll be taking over. Once you've met with Periscope, you can return directly to London."

He was bluffing. Or was it me who was? "I can't do that, and you know it."

Gus shook his head. "You can, but you won't."

I stood by the window, looking out at the view of the coos roaming Tag's land. "I don't know how to do this," I said when he stepped behind me and rested his hand on my shoulder.

"Just be, Ash. Let it happen on its own."

"There's more on my mind."

"Con?"

"Am I the only one who believes things aren't adding up?"

"Let's get this meeting over with and see."

"Wait," I said when he walked to the door. "I appreciate this, Angus. Seeing that photo on my grandfather's bookshelf reminded me what a good friend you've been all my life."

"Likewise, Ashcroft."

12

Sullivan

"There he is," said Con, who'd taken the seat to my right while Tag sat on my left. David sat across from me.

"Where would you like to start?" he asked, looking between Con and me.

"Tag mentioned a data breach at Crown Herald," I said, anxious to hear about Con's meeting with the new editor in chief, who I'd yet to meet.

"It was extensive," Con began, explaining that, upon closer inspection, whoever had hacked into the servers was looking for anything and everything to do with Eric Weber and Tower-Meridian.

"Most of what I'd actually uploaded was backed up elsewhere." What I didn't say was I'd never put the majority of my work on any of the news agency's servers. "When I last spoke with my editor, he said Ms. Wallace told him to shut down the investigation." I bit my lip. "So I removed it from the servers."

Con nodded. "They got it anyway. This was a sophisticated scrub, Sullivan." He drummed a stylus on the table. "What was that you said about shutting down your investigation? You said that edict came from your editor?"

"Clive Edwards, who you should probably know is also my uncle. I assure you that he had nothing to do with my getting the job, though."

"What are you thinking, Con?" David asked.

"Fallon didn't say anything about killing the investigation. Quite the contrary, actually."

"Elaborate," David pressed.

Con turned to face me. "She considers it very worthwhile, in fact. More so after the apparent hit taken out on you. She also said you're one of the best investigative journalists she's seen."

That stunned me. I was more used to criticism than praise. The other thing I'd gotten used to was the majority of the people I worked with not wanting to have anything to do with me. I knew they often went to the pub after work, even though I'd never once been invited to join them. I thought about showing up a time or two anyway, just to fuck with them, but never went through with it. Even Clive was stingy with any kind of praise or encouragement.

"In case you're questioning whether I'm being truthful with you, she'd welcome the opportunity to tell you herself."

I smiled, realizing I'd been shaking my head. "Not necessary, but thanks."

"I'd like to suggest we consider Weber's cyber capabilities equal to ours. At least in the interim until I can properly assess the threat level." From the corner of my eye, I saw him wink, but I knew from the security I'd seen thus far that he wasn't being facetious.

"Sullivan, would you be willing to brief the rest of the team on your investigation?" David asked.

I met his gaze. It was the first he'd looked at me since he returned to the dining room after being gone far longer than it should've taken him to retrieve his computer. Wanting to feel connected to him again, my eyes bored into his. I didn't answer or look away.

His eyes scrunched. "Sullivan?"

I nodded. "Yes. I will do."

"Ash, you're scheduled to meet with Periscope at fourteen hundred," said Gus, looking up from his mobile.

"Bloody hell," he said under his breath. "In order to do so, I need to leave in the next thirty minutes. Can you not—"

"No," Gus responded before David finished.

Would I sound childish if I said I wasn't comfortable discussing the details of my investigation without him present?

"Let's table Sullivan's briefing until you return," said Con, saving me from the embarrassment of saying it myself.

"Not necessary," said David.

"It is," I blurted, my eyes meeting his again.

"Very well," he said, his voice softening as though he was speaking only to me.

I longed to be alone with him, to feel his arms around me, to hear his reassurance, to know that, no matter what, he'd protect me. I wanted the David from last night, not the one he'd reverted to being this morning—cold, distant, and detached.

When he left the room, saying a collective good-bye to the group, I raised my chin and squared my shoulders, not wanting him to see the hurt I was experiencing. This wasn't any different than when the people I worked with shunned me. As for friends outside of the news agency, I'd lost touch years ago with anyone who might've been considered as such.

If David had been as demonstrative today as he was yesterday, there was a chance I would've been the one to withdraw. I was a loner. I lived alone, I worked on my own, and as far as a social life was concerned, I didn't have one. So how would he fit in my life anyway?

"Earlier, I said Ms. Wallace would welcome the opportunity to meet with you, Sullivan. Is that something you'd be happy to do?" Con asked.

"Of course."

"As it turns out, Fallon's family has a place on the Isle of Arran. If you'd like, I could make arrangements for her to visit today."

Today? "Um, sure, but I don't want to inconvenience her."

"She's looking forward to it."

I glanced over at Tag, who was studying his mobile. Based on the look on his face, it wasn't good.

"Is everything all right?" I asked, unable to help myself.

He glanced up at me. "Yes, fine."

I had to clench my fists hard enough that my fingernails dug into my palms to stop myself from calling him out on his expression. There was always a chance that whatever it was had nothing to do with me.

"Tag," said Con.

When we both raised our heads to look at him, he was motioning to me, chuckling.

"What?" I asked.

Con raised a brow, then said Tag's name a second time.

"No update on the intruders. We've been unable to track them."

"When will David return?" I asked, suddenly feeling impatient and antsy.

"I'm not sure he's even left," said Gus.

"Is there anything else we need to discuss at this time?" I asked.

"I don't believe so." Con looked between the two men, who shook their heads. "Only whether I should arrange the meeting with Ms. Wallace."

"Sure, and thanks." I pushed away from the table and left the room, but rather than going upstairs, I went into the library. I hadn't had time to explore it yesterday, but with David gone for several hours, doing so today would help keep my mind off when he'd return.

The Glenshadow library was among the most beautiful I'd ever seen. There were hundreds of books in the floor-to-ceiling shelves, comfy, oversized chairs were placed throughout the room, and plush, handwoven rugs kept the space as warm as the fireplace that was lit both yesterday and today. My favorite thing about it was the window seat that looked out over the loch. If I ever had a room such as this, it would be hard for me to leave even to sleep.

I stood by the window, clutching a throw pillow to my chest, and raised my face to the sun's warmth streaming in through the panes.

"It's a lovely spot."

I opened my eyes and spun around when I heard David's voice.

"It is," I said, turning back toward the window and placing the pillow where it had previously rested on the cushion.

He walked closer and stood beside me. "Not quite as nice as the library at Ashcroft, though."

"No? That's hard to even imagine."

"Sullivan?"

I wished I still held the pillow and could hug it tight to my chest. Perhaps then, the ache I felt from my overwhelming need to put my arms around him wouldn't hurt as much.

"I'm sorry."

I blinked away ridiculous tears and folded my arms. "No need."

"I wish I didn't have to return to Edinburgh today."

What could I say? That I wished he didn't have to, either?

"The good news is I won't be gone nearly as long as I thought. Gus was able to arrange for air transport. In fact, I believe I hear the helicopter arriving now."

The sound of blades got louder, and when I leaned forward, I saw it landing on the lawn below.

"I should be on my way."

"Safe travels," I said, still unable to look at him for fear my every insecurity would play out on my face.

"When I return, we should talk."

I bristled but nodded. "Of course," I mumbled, wishing I had the option of leaving before he got back so I could avoid the inevitable letdown he planned to deliver.

"Bye, David," I said, turning in the opposite direction and walking over to the closest bookshelf.

I felt him behind me, close enough that if I leaned back just slightly, my body would rest against his.

"This is, err, unfamiliar territory for me. I, uh, that's to say, I'm not one who has ever…" he stammered.

"Me either," I whispered.

He put his hands on my shoulders and spun me around. "The connection I feel between us may be something I've made more of than it really is." He smiled and touched my cheek with his fingertip. "As my three closest friends would attest, I fancied myself quite smitten with you when we were children. Silly, I suppose."

"Not silly."

"You're being kind."

I shook my head.

He groaned and looked up at the ceiling. "I've really got to go."

"As you said, we'll talk when you return."

"There's just one thing."

My gaze met his.

"I want to kiss you."

I'd expected a quick and chaste buss, but when his tongue pressed against my lips, I wrapped my arms around his neck and opened to him.

He pulled away when his phone vibrated several times.

"You have to go," I said before he could.

"Actually, the message is for you. Apparently, Con had the pilot stop on the Isle of Arran on his way here to get me."

My eyes opened wide. "Ms. Wallace is already here?" I smoothed my hair and glanced down at what I was wearing, relieved when I remembered the clothes Mrs. Drummond—or whoever—had arranged for me were far nicer than anything I owned.

David took my hand. "Come, walk with me. Wait, you're shaking," he said, looking down at our fingers, woven with each other's.

"I've not met her."

"Should I tell you she already thinks you're brilliant?"

I rolled my eyes and gently pulled my hand from his.

"Right. Meeting the boss. Should be professional," he muttered.

I stopped walking and put my hand on his arm. "I hope it goes well with Periscope."

"I'll admit this is not a meeting I'm anxious to attend. However, if it gets us some answers, it will be worth it." He sighed and put his hand on top of mine. "Answers for you, Sullivan."

David and I kissed once more before we rounded the corner where Con was waiting with Ms. Wallace, Tag, and Gus. I was stunned by how young she looked. I'd seen a photo, but in it, she appeared a decade older than she did in person.

"Fallon, this is Ash," said Con when David stepped forward.

"It's a pleasure to meet you. Forgive my abrupt departure, but my ride awaits."

The woman smiled. "I'm aware I delayed your travels. Apologies," she said before turning to me. "You must be Sullivan."

"I am. It's an honor to meet you, Ms. Wallace." From the corner of my eye, I saw David walk out to the waiting helicopter.

She extended her hand, and we shook. "Please call me Fallon."

"Yes, ma'am."

She smiled. "Fallon."

My cheeks flushed, and I grinned.

"Is there somewhere private we can chat?" she asked.

I looked at Tag. "Wherever you'd like," he offered.

"The library is my favorite room in Glenshadow."

"I already know it will be mine as well. I'm also most at home in a room full of books."

"Can I bring you anything?" Tag asked.

"Tea would be lovely." Fallon linked her arm through mine as we walked away. "We have much to discuss," she added.

"Of course. I expect you'll want an overview of the Tower-Meridian investigation."

"Before you do so, my understanding is that Clive Edwards—"

"My uncle." My cheeks flushed. "Apologies for the interruption."

"Of course. Anyway, according to Blackmoor, he told you I wanted the investigation shelved. I assure you I said nothing of the sort."

If she was telling the truth, it made the mystery of the conversation I'd overheard more curious. "There's more."

"Go on."

"I was on my way out of the office and went to wish him a happy Christmas when I heard him speaking to someone on what I guessed was his mobile. He said, 'I've done all I can. The rest is in your hands now.'"

Her eyes scrunched, and she approached the window. "Concerning," she muttered under her breath before turning to face me. "What do you think he was referring to?"

"As difficult as it is for me to accept as his niece, I can't help but wonder if he set me up."

Next, she asked how I learned Eric Weber would be attending an event at Edinburgh Castle, and when I told her about the alert that appeared on my computer, her eyes darkened.

"Have you brought this to anyone else's attention?" she asked.

"Not yet."

"Good. Let's keep it between you and me for now. In terms of updating me, I'm ready whenever you are."

"Of course."

"I sense hesitancy."

"I'd planned to brief everyone after David, err, Ash returned."

She raised a brow. "Yeah?"

My cheeks flushed again, and I couldn't hold back my grin, hard as I tried. "Can I ask you something?"

"Of course."

"How old are you?"

"Thirty-two."

My eyes opened wide.

"I suppose you're wondering how I made editor in chief so young."

"Not at all, actually."

"Good, given it's the same reason you're about to make executive editor of investigations at the age of twenty-eight."

I chuckled, but stopped when I realized she was serious.

"I'm, um, flattered."

Fallon shook her head. "You shouldn't be. In my opinion, it's overdue."

"Clive has years—"

"Because of Clive Edwards, you almost lost your life, Sullivan. If you're not clear on that fact, then I will rethink promoting you to his position. Thank God Ashcroft had the presence of mind to realize not all was as it seemed."

"I know you're right. It's just harder to accept, given he's my mother's brother."

"I understand." She reached over and squeezed my hand. "I must say, from what I know so far, you and I are going to make a fantastic team."

"You should know I'm not exactly well-liked in the department."

She smiled more broadly. "No? Well, the same is true of me in the entirety of the news agency."

"*I* like you."

"And I like you. Which is precisely why I believe we're going to bring this old boys' network to its knees."

"I hate to beat a dead horse, as they say, but you've just met me—"

She held up a hand. "I didn't need to meet you to recognize the caliber of your work."

"I appreciate it."

She looked around the room and rubbed her hands together. "Something tells me there's a treasure trove of information contained within these walls. Perhaps even something that will help us with the evil Eric Weber."

13

Savior

While on the flight to Edinburgh, I mentally prepared myself for my conversation with Periscope. I had two objectives, but only one worth pursuing. First, I wanted to determine for myself if she'd received the instructions to order me to shoot Sullivan directly from Weber.

Second was to convince her she wasn't a suspect, even though she was in custody. The idea that assigning the Tower-Meridian investigation to her would somehow lead us to Weber was ludicrous. Half of me had a mind to contact Typhon and tell him so.

I rested my head against the seat and glanced around the interior of the helicopter. Traveling to Edinburgh this way was a welcome luxury, one I could well afford but wouldn't have considered if Con hadn't made the suggestion.

Apart from the urgency of any given assignment, I was rarely in a hurry to get anywhere. Driving alone wasn't different than any other aspect of the way I chose to live my life. Now, I couldn't wait to return to Glenshadow and Sullivan.

Perhaps it would have been better to drive. I would have had time to sort through my feelings for her. And then what? I wasn't lying when I said this thing between us was new for me. What good would over-thinking it do?

There'd been women in my life, of course, but considering my line of work, I'd never been in a relationship. It wouldn't have been possible unless it was with someone either in MI6 or Unit 23 who already knew I was an assassin. While it was common among my fellow agents to have affairs and even marry, there wasn't anyone I worked with who I wanted to have a drink with, let alone shag.

With Sullivan, I wanted her in every way—in my bed and in my life. I'd be happy just having her in my arms. I closed my eyes, reliving every moment of the morning, from giving her the cold shoulder to knowing I couldn't leave Glenshadow without attempting to make things right between us. Not that I had done. At least not entirely.

All too soon, yet not soon enough, I felt our descent and rolled my shoulders, dreading the conversation ahead and knowing I couldn't be benevolent toward Periscope. Assassins weren't empathetic. At least none I knew.

"Typhon? I didn't expect to see you," I said after coming inside from the helipad and finding him leaning up against the wall.

"I've not much time," he said as we approached the building's security checkpoint. "By the way, we're on high-alert protocol."

"Right, err…" I scrunched my eyes. "Why are you here?" I asked once I'd surrendered my weapons.

"Periscope."

If he were taking the meeting in my place, I'd be greatly relieved. However, I doubted that was the case.

"I'll observe. Let's get this over with."

"Yes, sir."

I followed him to the lift, up a floor, then down the hall to an interview room I'd not previously been in.

"I'll forewarn you she's in a state. She's refusing to see or speak with anyone but you. When I attempted having a conversation with her, she became hysterical, saying she knew I was here to kill her. I suggested you had more reason to than I did."

"Did you, really?"

He nodded and motioned to a door. "Give me a couple of minutes, and I'll buzz you in. I want to see every reaction."

"Roger that," I responded, leaning up against the wall outside the room where Periscope waited. My question about whether Typhon had really said I had more reason to kill her than he did was rhetorical. Earlier, when I thought about the lack of empathy among those in my profession, my boss appeared at the top of that list.

At the same time my mobile pinged with an alert, the door unlocked and I entered.

"Periscope," I said when the woman I barely recognized raised her head. Her eyes were glassy, with dark circles beneath them, and her skin was ashen as if she hadn't seen sunlight in weeks rather than days. Her legs were shackled and her hands cuffed.

"Savior."

Hard as it was to remain detached, I reminded myself of two things. First and foremost, she was a traitor—an enemy within Unit 23's midst. As part of one of the most elite teams in the world, that someone had gotten to her was chilling in itself. Prior to this, I would've said we were impenetrable. "You demanded to speak with me."

"To warn you."

"Warn me about what?"

"They'll take you all out. Every one of you. First, me. Then, her. But they won't stop."

"Who, Shelby?"

"They're much more powerful than you think." Her eyes darted about.

"Why are you telling me this?"

Her eyes bored into mine. "I'm already dead. If only you'd killed her…"

"Do you think Weber would've let you live?" I scoffed, then sneered. "How did they get to you?"

"No one is safe. If you think you are, you're as stupid as I was. They'll come for you." She raised her brows as if something had occurred to her. "In fact, they already have."

My irritation with being here in the first place was exacerbated by her cryptic dialogue. Now, I was angry at what was evidently a bloody waste of time. "I see no point in continuing this conversation." I pushed my chair away from the table and stood.

"Janus thinks he controls Chimera. He's wrong. That may be your only chance at survival." She looked at the door that she'd likely been brought in through. "I have nothing more to say."

As soon as I reached the door I'd come in, the lock clicked. Typhon waited right outside.

"She's delirious," I muttered.

"Yet the information she gave may be of value."

"Janus and Chimera?"

"What is it they say? Keep your friends close and your enemies closer?"

I glanced around to make sure we were alone. "What are you suggesting, Typhon?"

"Come with me." He stepped into another room and shut the door behind us. "She said, 'they already have.' Whoever is coming for you is already in your midst, Savior."

"That Weber got to me through Periscope tells you that the unit is vulnerable."

He paced the room, something I often did. "We need to assess everyone."

I put my hands on my hips, looked down at the floor, and shook my head. "I won't do it. Don't bother asking."

"Even to save Sullivan's life?"

"If you have reason to believe anyone in my crew, as you call us, is dirty, spell it out for me right now. If you're grasping at something that isn't there because of a warning given to us by a madwoman, you can fuck off."

He put his hand on the doorknob. "Once the seed of doubt is planted, there's nothing to stop it from growing."

"You're a bloody bastard, Marras."

He shrugged his shoulder. "You should be thanking me that you still have a job, Ashcroft."

"Until I find the next traitor you let in the gate. Then, what?"

He grinned but not through his eyes. "Maybe I'll retire and let you take over. In the meantime, I'll run the names Janus and Chimera and see if anything relevant pops up."

By the time the helicopter landed at Glenshadow, I was ready to tear Con limb from limb. I was equally angry with myself for not having the conversation I'd told myself I would prior to meeting with Periscope.

"Where's Con?" I asked when I was met at the door by Tag and Gus.

"Ashcroft," said Tag.

"I need to speak with him immediately."

"I'll drive you over," Tag offered.

I shook my head. "This is between Con and me alone."

Gus handed me a key fob.

"Where is Sullivan?"

"She and Fallon Wallace are in the library," Gus responded.

"Find her, and do not let her out of your sight until I return."

Tag followed when I stormed outside. "What's going on, Ash?"

"My apologies, my friend, but I must sort this with Con first."

Typhon was right about there being nothing to stop the seed of doubt from growing once planted. Right now, Con was on my radar. That didn't mean Tag or even Gus weren't the person, or persons, who'd come for me. I'd give almost anything to have every suspicion quashed, to believe without the shadow of a doubt that my three closest friends would never betray me or the Crown. Except the one thing—person—I could not risk in this was Sullivan. It was my responsibility to protect her, and if called for, I'd lay down my life to save hers.

"I'm looking for Con," I said when Mrs. Drummond met me just inside the entrance to the castle.

"He's at Thistle Gate."

I was almost out the door when I heard her call after me.

"Your Grace, if I may."

"Time and again, I've told you not to address me in that manner, Mrs. Drummond."

Since I hadn't stopped walking, she hurried after me. "Understood, sir, but…"

I sighed. "Yes?"

"Your uncle has returned."

My father's doddering brother was the least of my worries at the moment. I stopped walking and turned to her. "And?"

She stepped closer and lowered her voice. "Lord Blackmoor said he believed you may be returning to the estate later today."

"I urgently need to speak with *Con*, as I'll point out, you've referred to him for most of our lives. After which, I will return and speak with you."

"Thank you, your—"

I leveled a glare at her.

"Ash."

"That's better." I stalked off toward the bridge, but before I'd managed to get across, I heard Ambrose shouting my name.

"David, a word?" he hollered.

"Not fucking now, Brose," I muttered, not loud enough for him to hear me. Instead, I waited for him to meet me where I stood.

"Hello, Uncle. I didn't expect you."

He opened his mouth, then shut it, then opened it again. "I'll remind you that Ashcroft is my home as much as it is yours," he sputtered.

While I wanted to inform him that it wasn't and that I'd been generous in allowing him to come and go as he pleased, I had no time and even less inclination to get into an argument with him.

"I have an urgent matter to attend to and will speak with you once that's taken care of. Goodbye, Ambrose."

"But, but…" I heard him continue sputtering as I hurried off in the direction of Thistle Gate. As I rounded the front of the cottage, Con came out the front door.

"Hey, Ash. What happened with Periscope?"

"Before I answer that question, I have one for you."

His brow furrowed at my tone. "Shall we go inside?"

"Let's take a walk instead."

Not far from the cottage, outside my estate's perimeter, there was an old pier. While I didn't doubt there was surveillance of some kind picking up our activity, I hoped that what the two of us said to one another wasn't.

"Ash? What's going on?"

"What do you know about Tower-Meridian's business?"

He sat on one of the pilings. "Why don't you cut to the chase and ask me what you really want to know?"

"Very well. How is it one of the world's preeminent cyber experts was unaware of the true nature of his business?"

Con looked out at the loch. "Until you asked me to look into Weber, he wasn't on my radar, Ash. He wasn't on anyone's, as far as I knew."

I studied him. Would I know if he was lying? Did I truly know him as well as I believed? Or had I turned such a blind eye to the activities he engaged in that it had gotten to the point where I ignored the possibility that, like Periscope, he could very well be a traitor?

When he got to his feet and stepped closer to where I stood near the end of the pier, my hackles raised.

"Ashcroft."

I faced him. "Blackmoor."

"I will forgive you this as it's my fault you're doubting me in the first place. However, I swear on my mother's soul that I would never betray you or the Crown. Now, what's going on? Just be straight with me, for fuck's sake."

Con didn't waver nor did he step away. He had every right to punch me in the face and knock me into the loch. And yet, he stood toe-to-toe with me, barely blinking, let alone looking away.

"Periscope."

"I figured that much. What did she say?"

I motioned to the pilings. "A lot of rambling, but she mentioned two names—Janus and Chimera."

He shook his head. "Not immediately familiar."

"Typhon is running them."

He smirked. "As will I when we're finished. Is your line of questioning the reason he hasn't asked me to do it yet?"

"He muttered something about seeds of doubt taking root." He still hadn't looked away, but I did. "Periscope is certain Weber is going to get to her. She said, 'No one is safe. If you think you are, you're as stupid as I was. They'll come for you.' Then she added as if she suddenly realized something, 'In fact, they already have.'"

"I see. So she's suggesting there's a traitor in our midst in addition to her."

"She also said, 'Janus thinks he controls Chimera. He's wrong. That may be your only chance at survival.'"

"Tell me what you know about Weber. What's he into?"

"Sullivan's theory is weapons trafficking, yet I can't help but wonder why he'd order a hit on a reporter if that were the case."

"So, it's worse." He put one hand on his hip. "I'll admit one of the reasons I came over here was how hard it was for me not to eavesdrop on her and Fallon. And, no, Ash, I didn't plant any ears."

"I'm sorry for doubting you, Con."

He half nodded, half shook his head. "I'm more than miffed, but as I said, I've given you cause through the years to doubt me." He hesitated, but I sensed there was more he wanted to say. A few seconds later, he did. "I've been better of late, you know. Not that any of my more nefarious activities, as you and Tag called them, were criminal in nature."

"I've no right to criticize you. I knew full well you'd employ means not necessarily sanctioned by SIS when I asked you to find all you could on Weber and Tower-Meridian."

"Is anything Unit 23 does sanctioned?"

We both chuckled.

"The person whose brain I really want to pick is Sullivan's."

"You and me both." I glanced back at the cottage. "How far off are we from returning?"

"Not as close as I thought we'd be. I discovered industrial-strength malware on the Crown Herald's servers. I have to hand it to Fallon. One of the first things she did after coming on board at the agency was to put a cyber-resilience system in place."

"How complex?"

"Critical infrastructure in line with GCHQ's cyber-security guidance protocols."

I was stunned, but more, I couldn't help but wonder if we should be taking a closer look at Fallon Wallace's background.

"I dug deep," said Con, picking up on my train of thought.

"And?"

"Better if I let her tell you herself. I'll say this much. I'll sleep better at night knowing both she and Sullivan are on our side." I opened my mouth, but he held up his hand. "And, yes, I do believe they are firmly on the side of good, not evil."

I sighed again and looked up at the castle. "Brose is back."

Con rolled his eyes. "I *know*."

"What makes you say it that way?"

"Can't you deny him access? I finally had to escort the bugger out of the cottage. I swear, if I hear one more story about your grandfather, who your uncle is convinced would've made him the heir over your dad if the Crown would've allowed it, I'll lose my bloody mind."

"There's been more than one occasion when I wished I could do the same. The man has no idea what it takes to run an estate of this magnitude."

Con chuckled. "I'd blame inbreeding again, but you turned out all right."

14

Sullivan

David had returned from Edinburgh, then left almost immediately after exiting the helicopter. Even from the window seat, I could sense his anger through his body language alone.

Fallon and I decided, at my insistence, that we'd wait for his return to discuss our individual efforts in the Tower-Meridian investigation.

Instead, we focused on the changes she'd been implementing behind the scenes at the Crown Herald. While I'd kept the bulk of my research off the main servers, I wasn't naive enough to think my own computer was secure. In fact, it was far less so. I supposed a part of me believed I could fly far enough under the radar that no one would be looking. It was a ridiculously stupid supposition in light of what was intended to be my murder.

When she mentioned the UK's National Cyber Security Centre—or NCSC—I admitted to having heard of it. What stunned me was that she'd worked with them on the cybersecurity protocols that had protected our research from the massive data breach that occurred simultaneously with my arrival at Edinburgh Castle.

The media's relationship with any government entity was tenuous in the best of circumstances. The mandate of news agencies, at least the ones who still practiced ethics in journalism, was to inform the public of issues that would affect their lives. Governments strove to keep those same issues out of the press entirely. Theoretical independence was tested on a daily basis with conflicts often playing out through legal injunctions, public criticism, restricted access to officials, or threats of prosecution under the Official Secrets Act.

Agencies that operated under the umbrella of SIS, such as the ones David and his friends worked for, were particularly under threat of exposure. Case in point, David aka the Duke of Ashcroft, was a bloody assassin. If outed, not only would the Crown face criticism and scrutiny, but he'd have a target on his back for the rest of his life.

I understood the threat the media represented not just to him but anyone in government, all too well. Journalists would do anything to protect their sources and refused to turn a blind eye when it came to political scandals. Classified information was leaked either in an attempt to raise subscription rates via sensationalism, whether it be online or in print, or under the guise of whistleblowing. What few comprehended were the moral and ethical dilemmas we regularly faced. I truly believed the majority of people who chose to pursue a career in my profession had no interest in exploitative journalism. Another way I supposed I was naive.

"Sullivan? A hand?"

I looked over to where Fallon precariously balanced on top of a rolling ladder while she attempted to reach a rather large book from the highest shelf.

"Why couldn't I have inherited my father's genes and grown beyond five feet four?" she muttered, standing on tiptoes. I'd offer to get it, but I was only an inch taller.

"What are you after?" I asked.

"What appears to be monastery records. Ancient ones. The entire shelf is lined with them."

"Is there a good reason you wouldn't want to request assistance?" I asked.

"Of course there is. Climb up and spot me."

"Got you," I said, placing one hand on her waist. Honestly, I doubted I was any help at all. If she toppled over, I'd likely go with her.

"Success," she said, handing the volume to me. "I think I might be able to reach another."

"Or die trying," I muttered.

"Come now, Sullivan. Where's your spirit of adventure?"

"Having come close to death once this week, I'm hesitant to tempt fate twice."

"Shall I save you a second time?" I heard David say from behind me.

I turned and smiled. "This time, it's Fallon who needs your assistance."

He walked over to the ladder and took the heavy book from my hands, then held his free one out to help me down.

"What are you after up there?" he asked Fallon, who hesitated to accept his assistance once my feet were firmly planted on the floor.

"History has always intrigued me," she said, abandoning the second tome she already had her hand on. "I can't resist once I spot something that looks remotely ancient."

David set the book on the table and stood by the ladder when Fallon made her way down.

"It's a silly fascination, really," she said under her breath.

"So, you're back," I said, attempting to distract David from looking at the book he'd placed on the table. While it may contain nothing significant, my gut, along with Fallon's level of interest, told me it might.

He sighed. "I am that."

"Did you learn anything of value?" I asked.

"I might have done. Too soon to tell."

I folded my arms out of reflex. Did he really believe I'd brief him, Con, Tag, and Gus without him sharing information with me?

"I've been sent to see if you're ready to meet," he said, looking from me to Fallon.

"Of course," she responded. "I'll just gather my things."

"We'll join you shortly," I said, in effect, dismissing him.

For a moment, I thought he intended to wait for us, but after nodding once, he left the room.

"I need to hide this," Fallon said, lifting the record book from the table.

"Why? What's in it?"

"I don't know yet, but something tells me if our host knew of my interest, it, along with the others, would disappear."

"Here," I said, walking over to the window seat. "I noticed a hidden storage area beneath the cushion yesterday."

She raised a brow and smirked. "You *noticed* it?"

I raised my chin but smiled. "In the same way you did what we intend to hide."

"Touché. Is there anything inside?" she asked when I lifted the hinged cover.

"I haven't looked."

She chuckled. "Liar."

I laughed too, but I hadn't since, right after I noticed it, David had walked in.

She placed the book inside while I held the cover open. "Did you see that?" she asked, pointing at another set of hinges. However, there was no handle on the cut-out that appeared painted shut. "Later," she whispered.

I nodded, replaced the cushion, and gathered my things.

When Fallon and I entered the dining room, we noticed it had been transformed into what one might see on a detective drama TV series.

"Wow," I said under my breath, taking in the electronic evidence boards.

"We're locked up tight," said Con when I took one of the open seats. "Meaning the highest level security protocols have been implemented. What you share in this room stays in this room. The same is expected of the two of you. If you cannot agree or are unwilling to sign an NDA, then this meeting ends before it begins."

"And will you do the same?" Fallon asked.

"Of course," Con responded. "We see this as an opportunity for collaboration. One that could benefit us all individually but also the agencies we represent."

Fallon, who'd also taken a seat, folded her arms and rested them on the table. "Let's not get ahead of ourselves."

I glanced at David, who was studying me. Was he waiting for me to balk? If I did, then what? I could hardly venture out on my own, even with support from the Crown Herald, especially now that the ramifications of Weber's capabilities were becoming more apparent.

"I've sent both of you the NDA draft. Once you've had the chance to review it, we'll all sign one physical copy."

Considering the meeting could not commence until we'd done so, I pulled up the document on my computer and began reading. No doubt Fallon had far more experience with agreements of this nature and would spot things I'd miss.

While brief, the terms seemed concise. The paragraph that defined what constituted confidential information was the lengthiest as it detailed all forms of information that would be covered, including both written and verbal details, digital and physical documents, and intellectual property.

The rest outlined specific permissible uses, exclusions and exceptions—or that there weren't any—and duration and termination. Beyond that, each person in the room was listed by name, along with their respective entities.

"I'm good with this," said Fallon, raising her head and looking over at me.

"As am I."

"Good. Let's get to work." Con signed the physical copy of the document first, then passed it to Fallon, who was seated to his right. After she skimmed it, she signed it, then passed it to David.

Apart from Con, the overall mood in the room was somber.

"Before we get started, I have an update on yesterday's security breach," said Tag, the last to sign.

"Go ahead," said Con.

"A combination of measures designed to interfere with GPS tracking were utilized. Drones were used to create electromagnetic interference while localized jammers served as backup to keep the intruders' presence undetectable. Finally, sensors picked up on heat signatures that, in essence, were decoys."

"Thus, the overheads were ineffective," said David.

"If anyone has any doubt about the sophistication of what we're dealing with, think again," Con added.

"And, just in case all that failed, footage inside Glenshadow's surveillance was looped and false data planted."

David got up from the table and walked over to the window. "How soon can we return to Ashcroft?"

"Twenty-four to forty-eight hours," answered Con.

"And in the meantime?"

"We're working on our systems concurrently," said Tag.

David's mouth gaped.

"The timetable isn't nearly as long," Tag added.

"What about Blackmoor?"

"The same," said Con. "However, I'll remind you that before this meeting began, I told each of you that the highest-level security protocols have been implemented. What that means is our scrambling capabilities are equal or better than theirs."

"Fucking hell. Anyone capable of doing what Weber's done this far certainly knows where to hit next." He turned to me. "We're leaving."

Gus stood. "Ash, hold on—"

"I said we're leaving. The matter is not open for discussion."

"I'll, um, get my things together," I said, pushing my chair back.

"I'll help," Fallon offered.

"Ash, they cannot hit us again," I heard Con say, but rather than listen to the rest, I went upstairs.

"Wow," said Fallon when she followed me into the suite. "Nice setup."

"Truthfully, it's too much space for me."

She raised a brow. "Clearly, you had no princess fantasies as a child."

"In this case, it would be a countess."

"Right," she said while I took items of clothing out of the closet and placed them in the suitcase David had requested be brought to me when we left Ashcroft.

"If we hadn't already signed an NDA, I'd assign you this story. A duke and two earls, all part of the SIS' most secretive and elite unit."

"I'd turn you down."

She chuckled. "Not hard-hitting enough for you, Sullivan?"

"Some things are better left to the unknown."

She sat on the edge of the bed. "You trust them, then?"

"Enough that I was prepared to brief them on my investigation."

"Where do you suppose you're off to?"

I shook my head. "I've no idea." I walked over to my laptop bag, pulled out the pocket knife I kept inside, and cut along the seam of the bottom. I reached between two pieces of cardboard and removed a third. Affixed to it was a microSD card.

"Sullivan?" Fallon gasped. "Are you certain you're ready to hand this off?"

I nodded. "It's all here. Well, everything that isn't in here." I pointed to my head. "I'll be interested to see what you make of it."

"What do you want me to do with this?"

"Review it in the safest place you can find. Then brief them if you're comfortable doing so."

"Not without you, I won't."

"The choice is yours. However, time may force your hand."

She nodded. "Understood, and hurry back, Sullivan. I'm anxious to continue our exploration of Glenshadow's library."

15

Savior

"Scramble everything at Ashcroft as well," I said to Con before turning to Gus. "Kindly arrange helicopter transport."

"To?" he asked.

"I'll let you know as soon as I've spoken to Typhon."

"Copy that."

"That's where you're off to, then?" Tag asked.

"Since I don't yet know where I'm going, I don't see how you would."

"Ash, come on—"

I spun around on Con. "Do not even think about talking me out of this." I turned to Gus and Tag. "In my meeting with Periscope, she said, 'They'll come for you. In fact, they already have.' I will not sit by, knowing whatever security we have in place isn't good enough to protect Sullivan." I shook my head. "I cannot," I added under my breath.

"You were going to contact Typhon," said Gus, standing and walking over to me.

"Right." I looked over at Con.

"You're clear to communicate with whomever you'd like. As I already said, everything's been jammed since Tag gave us his report."

"Thanks." I pulled out my mobile.

"I'll see what I can do to tighten the schedule at Ashcroft," Con added.

"Appreciated."

I stepped out of the room and placed my call.

"I need to relocate Sullivan Rivers immediately."

"You've heard, then?"

"Heard what?"

"They found Periscope about an hour ago."

"Cause of death?" I asked.

"Unknown. The medical examiner is working on it now."

"She said she was already dead."

"Poison?"

"Definitely a possibility."

"Where do you want to go?" Typhon asked.

"The safest place you can find."

"Got it. I'll arrange transport."

"This isn't just about me wanting to protect Sullivan. Whatever she knows, whether aware of it or not, is enough that they'll not stop until they silence her."

"Understood."

"I appreciate this, sir."

"Just remember this when it's your turn."

I shook my head. "No way in hell I'd take your job, Marras."

"You're a smarter man than I was. Oh, and for the time being, Orion is your handler."

It had been so long since I'd heard anyone use Gus' official code name that I'd forgotten it.

"And you're inactive."

If I had my say, I'd remain that way permanently, not that I'd initiate that dialogue now. All I cared about presently was getting Sullivan somewhere where Weber couldn't get his hands on her.

"Typhon's arranged for transport," I told Gus when I returned to the room after ending the call.

"Copy that."

"He relayed more news."

Both Con and Tag raised their heads.

"Periscope?" Gus asked.

"They found her about an hour ago."

"COD?" he asked.

"Unknown." I turned to Con again. "I want Ashcroft locked up tighter than Vauxhall Cross before I'll even consider returning."

"Understood."

"Gus, make contact with Typhon. Regardless of where we're headed, even if it is SIS's headquarters, I want security teams in place around the clock."

"Roger that."

"Anything else?"

"What does she know, Ash?" Tag asked.

"I wish I knew. I'm not sure even she does."

"Maybe it's time we found out," Con suggested.

"My first priority is her safety."

"Understood. However, if whatever they're doing is big enough that Weber will risk everything to get to her, then we bloody well better find out what it is."

I went upstairs, and when I passed Sullivan's room, I overheard her and Fallon speaking.

"What do you want me to do with this?" Fallon asked.

"Review it in the safest place you can find. Then brief them if you're comfortable doing so."

"Not without you, I won't."

"The choice is yours. However, time may force your hand."

I rapped on the door and entered without being bidden. "What is that?" I asked, motioning to the piece of cardboard Fallon held in her hand.

"There's a microSD card attached," Sullivan responded.

"My apologies, but would you please give that to me?"

"I beg your pardon?" Sullivan said. Fallon, on the other hand, held it out to me.

"Periscope is dead. We don't yet know the cause, but someone got to her. Whatever is on that card, whatever you've uncovered about Tower-Meridian, whoever possesses that knowledge will have a target on their back." I faced Sullivan and looked into her eyes. "Do you understand?"

"I do."

"Transport is on the way, and when they arrive, we'll depart." I turned to Fallon. "While Con assures me Glenshadow is airtight in terms of what we discussed, my belief is that Weber is able to assess our current vulnerabilities and act on them. That you were here at all already makes you a target.

"What do you suggest?" she asked.

"Protection."

She nodded. "Understood."

"Will you excuse us?" I asked.

"Of course." Fallon walked out the door and shut it behind her.

"Forgive my intrusion—" I began, but stopped when Sullivan covered her face with her hands.

"No need to apologize. I didn't realize…"

"What have you uncovered, Sully?" I asked after putting my arms around her.

"I wish I knew," she said, resting her cheek against my shoulder.

Once we arrived wherever Typhon was sending us, I'd ask her to share the contents of the card with me. It would be up to Sullivan whether she trusted me enough to do so.

The helicopter that arrived on Tag's estate was different from the one I'd taken to Edinburgh. The pilot was someone I recognized from Unit 23.

"Savior," he said when we got in.

"Osprey," I responded, wondering if Sullivan had picked up on his use of my code name. No doubt she had.

We went as far as the private airfield in Glasgow, where we boarded a private plane also owned by Unit 23.

"Hello, Angel," I said when we boarded and I saw her in the cockpit. She often flew with an American pilot who was a contractor for the unit. "Is Crash with you today?" I asked.

"No. Condor, who hasn't yet arrived, will be copiloting." I'd never met her or him, but Angel was clearly not pleased about their tardiness. Given my current state of high anxiety, neither was I.

"Sullivan, this is Teagon, who as I'm sure you heard, we call Angel."

After the two women shook hands, I led Sullivan into the cabin. "Do you have a preference as to where we sit?" I asked.

"You're kidding, yes?"

I cocked my head.

"I'll confess I've never traveled via private plane, so no, I do not have a preference."

"One grows to take it for granted, I suppose." Particularly given when I had occasion to make use of it, it was to carry out an assignment.

I chose captain's chairs in the middle of the cabin.

"So, Savior?"

I half smiled. "Caught that, did you?"

"Interesting code name, although I have considered you mine."

I wasn't one to embarrass easily nor would anyone describe me as particularly humble. Sullivan's words made me feel both.

"Have I thanked you for saving my life?" she asked, resting her hand on my arm.

"More than once, err, I mean, thanked me."

"He's arrived," Angel said from the front of the plane. "Once we're in the air, flight time will be approximately ninety minutes. Feel free to help your-selves to what's in the galley."

"Would you like anything? Something to drink or eat?" I asked after thanking Angel.

"Whatever you're having."

I typically refrained from having anything on my way to an assignment. Afterwards, I had two fingers of bourbon, neat. While I was certain there were plenty of offerings, I had no idea what they might be. "Shall we take a look?" When I stood and held out my hand, Sullivan took it. Without releasing it, I led her to the front of the plane just as the copilot arrived.

"Hello," the man with an American accent said.

I nodded once but didn't respond, nor did I intro-duce him to Sullivan.

"Charcuterie, more charcuterie, and a wide range of beverages, including my favorite bourbon."

"That sounds quite good, actually."

I poured two glasses. "Ice?" I asked.

Her eyes widened. "And water it down? Never."

I chuckled. "A woman after my own heart." Not that she didn't already own it. Given I hadn't eaten much in the last few days and doubted Sullivan had either, I also brought two charcuterie trays to our seats.

"Based on travel time, my guess is we're on our way to London. From there, I've no idea."

She'd just popped a piece of cheese in her mouth, so she nodded in response.

"I'm a bit surprised you haven't asked."

Her cheeks flushed. "I'm learning."

I rested my head against the seat and gazed at her. "I like your inquisitive nature. I always have."

"Coming as close as I did to dying has tempered my curiosity."

"Don't let Weber win."

Her eyes opened wider. "You're right."

Like she had in the SUV, Sullivan fell asleep almost immediately. Having her head on my shoulder felt like the most natural thing in the world. Any discomfort I felt when with her was my own forced doing. And why? Hadn't I already stopped myself too many times from allowing people to get close to me? If it weren't for Gus, Con, and Tag, I'd have no friendships or relationships outside of work. And while I did work with them, that we'd known each other since childhood made it different.

I silently vowed not to allow myself to push Sullivan away nor would I allow her to do the same to me. At the very least, I wanted us to be friends. Ideally, far more.

When my phone vibrated, I pulled it from my pocket as gingerly as I could so as not to disturb her. The message I received was from Typhon, saying we'd be transported to his flat once our flight landed and that standard entry procedures used for SIS had been activated. Given his place served as one of the Unit 23 command centers, it probably had security systems in place that rivaled Vauxhall Cross—or better. As far as somewhere I felt confident Sullivan would be safe, I couldn't have come up with a better idea.

Much appreciated, I responded.

In town. Will arrange to meet.

Copy that, I responded, not that I was anxious to do so. In fact, given the close proximity to the holidays, I was hoping Sullivan and I could spend it quietly, just the two of us.

Something told me the weeks that followed would be anything but tranquil.

"Hello," I said when I realized Sullivan's eyes were open and she was staring up at me.

"I fell asleep."

I leaned down and kissed her temple. "You did."

"What were you thinking about?"

"You."

"Good or bad thoughts?"

"Always good."

She raised a brow as though she didn't buy it.

"It's the truth."

"Why?"

If her expression wasn't so serious, I may have chuckled. Instead, I touched the tip of her nose with my index finger. "Is it so hard to believe I like everything about you?"

"No one else does," she said under her breath. "In fact—"

I silenced her with a kiss, and when she tried to pull away, I cupped her cheek. "Perhaps I'm the only one who truly knows you."

"While that's very sweet. I would include my parents in my blanket statement."

"How much of the real you do you let them see?"

Her eyes darted between mine. "Likely very little."

I wove my fingers with hers. "We'll be landing soon." I waited several seconds to see if she'd ask where we'd go from there, but she didn't. I found myself disappointed. "You're taking the fun out of this adventure."

She leaned back. "I thought you said you liked everything about me."

"I'm teasing."

"Where are we staying, Davy?" she asked in a voice that sounded more like her eight-year-old self.

"You'll see."

When she slugged my arm, I laughed.

Typhon's place was much like I'd pictured it. In fact, it reminded me of my flat, here in the city. I'd purchased it furnished, kept nothing personal in it, and was rarely there. Perhaps after he'd married, he'd taken mementos with him. Or, like me, he had none.

"This is, err, nice," Sullivan said once we were inside.

"It belongs to my boss."

"It's, um, very modern."

I chuckled. "It's also cold." I walked over and flipped a switch that, as I'd expected, lit a gas fireplace. "There are three bedrooms, I believe. Take your pick."

"It doesn't matter to me. Wherever you'd be most comfortable. Wait. I mean, pick the one where you would be."

I stepped closer to her. "I like your first idea better."

She rubbed her arms. "I don't think the chill has much to do with the temperature. It's the overall feel of the place."

"If it helps, I don't believe he spends time here anymore. He was recently married."

Sullivan walked over to the windows in the main room. "It has a lovely view."

I looked down at what was one of my favorite pubs in the city, hating that I wouldn't feel comfortable taking Sullivan there. Which reminded me that I hadn't followed up with Gus about the protection I requested to be put into place. I sent him a message asking for confirmation.

"For someone who doesn't live here, he keeps his refrigerator well stocked."

I hadn't noticed Sullivan walking away. "Hungry?" I asked, joining her in the kitchen that was twice the size of the one in my flat.

"Not really?"

"A drink?" I suggested.

"Sure."

I noticed a wine cooler beneath the counter. "Fancy a glass?"

She shook her arms like they were noodles. "Something stronger might be better. I feel so…"

"Uncomfortable?"

"I'm sorry. It's just so utilitarian. And before you say it, I know I should just be grateful to be alive, not complaining about my accommodations. It's just that, never mind."

I pulled her over to the sofa where we could sit near the fire. "Tell me."

"I was most comfortable at the cottage. It felt like"—she shrugged—"you, I guess. The suite at Tag's was lovely…God, I sound so ungracious."

"The suite was lovely, but…"

"It was so big, no?"

I smiled. "Castles can be that way."

"Do you spend much time at yours?" She snuggled closer to me, and I put my arm around her.

"I haven't done. As I said, I don't spend time any-where, really. What about you?"

"If I'm not at the office, I'm home. I don't really go anywhere else."

"Tell me what it's like."

She raised a brow.

"Come on. Play along."

That made her laugh out loud. "Well, it's a bit of a mess, typically. I'm sure you find that *very* surprising."

"Tell me your favorite thing about it." When her cheeks flushed, I was even more intrigued. "Come on. What is it?"

"My bed."

I nuzzled her neck. "I have a strong suspicion it would be my favorite thing too."

"David?"

"Too much?" I asked, removing my hand from where I was caressing her shoulder.

Her breath caught. "Not enough."

"God, Sullivan. Do you know how much—"

She leaned up and caught my words with her mouth, and when our tongues met, it was like fire flowed through my veins with the ferocity of my desire.

The fevered kisses I trailed down the side of her neck were met by my hand that I had snaked under her blouse. When Sullivan reached up, unfastened the buttons, and pulled it open, I moved the cup of her bra out of my way and sucked her pink, hardened nipple.

I raised my eyes, making sure she felt the same intense desire I did. Her head was thrown back, her mouth open, and her fingers weaved in my hair.

"David," she gasped when I nipped her creamy flesh as I made my way to her other breast. Breathless moans escaped her lips when I cupped her mound with my palm. Feeling her wetness through her trousers made me need her naked—now.

I gathered her in my arms and carried her to the hallway, stopping at the first door I came to. When I kicked it open and saw a bed inside, it was all that mattered to me. I rested her on the mattress, then lay on top of her, nestled between her spread legs.

"I can feel how much you want me," she said, reaching between us to cup my shaft.

"And you, Sullivan? Do you want me too?"

"You know I do."

"Then, let me have you." I rolled to my side. "Undress for me." When she stood, I rolled to my back, put one arm behind my head, and watched as she leisurely, seductively, removed every stitch of clothing.

Once naked, she ran her hands over her bare skin, stopping to fondle her breast with one. When she reached between her legs, I was off the bed, grabbing both her wrists.

"You're driving me mad," I said, kneeling in front of her and spreading her legs before running my tongue through her folds. I couldn't remember being with any other woman, let alone one who kept herself bare. It made my already painfully hard cock rigid.

Sullivan wriggled her wrists from my hold and backed away. "Now, you." She lay where I'd been on the bed and, also like me, put one arm behind her head.

Unlike her, there was nothing languid about the way I tore my clothes from my body.

Once they were in a heap on the floor, I spread her legs and knelt between them. She reached for my cock, and I shuddered when she wrapped her hand around it.

"David, do you have a condom?" she asked, squeezing me until I almost came.

I reached over and pulled the beside table drawer open, saying a silent prayer of thanks when I saw an unopened box of them.

As much as I wanted my mouth on her, there'd be time for that later. All night. All day tomorrow. As often as she'd allow me, my mouth, my hands, my body would lavish her with the love I knew in my soul I felt for her, even when I knew I couldn't say the words.

I tore a foil packet open and observed her eyes as she watched me roll it on. That desire to see, to know, was one of the things I liked best. No—loved most.

"Please, David." She reached for me again, and I positioned myself at her entrance and eased into her tight channel. Her fingers dug into my arms, and the muscles of her legs that she'd wrapped around me stiffened. I stilled.

"Sullivan?" I said when I looked up and saw her face scrunched. "Am I hurting you?"

"No. It's just been a while."

"For me too."

She pried her eyes open and gazed into mine. "It was just the once."

I leaned down and kissed her, making love to her mouth with my tongue while I waited for her body to let me in. When I felt her pussy softening, I eased in a bit farther, then stilled again, keeping my eyes riveted to hers before reaching between us and fingering her clit.

"David?" I thrust into her, then withdrew before doing it again. "David?" she repeated.

"Yes, love?"

"I think, I mean, I'm going to…"

I increased my pace but restrained myself from going too hard and too deep, all the while gently rubbing her clit until she cried out, her body arching to take more of me as she repeated my name again and again.

I moved my finger and slowed but didn't withdraw, biding my time until I was certain she was ready for more. When she reached around and grabbed my arse, forcing me deeper inside, I let myself go. Knowing I wouldn't last much longer, I found her mouth, crashing into it with mine, wanting desperately to feel her kiss as I came. My cock pulsed, and I shuddered, knowing that, for the first time in my life, I'd made love. It was more than sex. It was love with the woman I'd spent years dreaming about.

16

Why had I told David I'd only been with a man once before? What must he be thinking about me now? That I was a loser who not only divided my time solely between work and home, but I also never had sex?

No friends. No lovers. No life. I certainly wasn't what one might consider a catch. Oh, and someone powerful enough to have an SIS agent killed while in custody also wanted me dead.

When David shifted, I thought for sure he'd get up, but instead, he wove his fingers in my hair and stared into my eyes. I'd never wanted to read someone's mind more than I did right now.

"Just say it."

His eyes scrunched, and his head cocked. "Say what? I mean, there are many things I'd like to say. I'm just wondering which you're so anxious to hear."

"I'm…you know."

"Sexy as fuck?"

His words were so unexpected that I laughed out loud. Then it dawned on me he was being sarcastic. "I know, right?"

He reached down, cupped my pussy, and inserted one finger inside me. "Sexy. As. Fuck."

My back arched when he added a second finger and pressed his thumb against my clit.

"I want you so much. I'm already hard as stone." He thrust deeper, and I clenched around his fingers. "Especially when you do that."

"I think it's a reflex," I said through gritted teeth.

"Let go."

"I'm not sure I know how."

"Not your pussy, your mind. Just feel, Sullivan. Let go and let yourself enjoy all the pleasure."

"I want to. I just…" He withdrew his fingers and got out of bed. "Wait. I'll try, okay?"

He smiled and shook his head. "Be right back."

I covered my face with my hand. "Oh. The condom."

As promised, he returned seconds later, moved the sheet that covered my body, and pulled my legs apart. "I love this," he said, running his fingers over my bareness, then spreading me open and licking from where his fingers had been inside me up to my clit. I jolted when his tongue swirled the ultra-sensitive bundle of nerves, but he used his opposite arm to hold me still.

"I can't," I groaned.

"You can and you will," he murmured. "I want you to come this way. Will you do that for me, Sullivan?"

I grabbed his shoulder, digging my nails into his flesh when the second orgasm crashed its way through me. I writhed on the bed as my pussy pulsed and my heart rate slowed down. He'd moved, but I didn't have the energy to even open my eyes to see where, until I heard him opening a foil packet.

I peeked as he rolled it on, then he pushed me to my side, positioned himself behind me, and raised my leg so it rested on his thigh. With one thrust, he entered me. "Oh my God," I cried as I felt yet another orgasm building.

When he touched my clit—just *touched* it—I came again, and as he moved inside me, rotating his hips and stroking my body in a place I never knew existed, I came again. This time, he did too.

"Don't move," he said, easing out of me to, as I now knew, dispose of the condom.

I grabbed the sheet and blanket to cover myself against the chill left by his absence. When he crawled in behind me, I snuggled against him. He wrapped his arm around me, and when he rested his hand on my pussy, I smacked it. "No."

He laughed. "Yes."

I stilled when his hand didn't move. He just cupped me. I felt myself drifting and shook myself awake.

"I love it when you sleep in my arms."

I glanced over my shoulder. "When have I?"

"On the plane, but more, in my dreams."

He kissed my shoulder, and a warmth like I'd never felt before spread throughout my body.

"Sleep, Sully," he whispered, and I did.

When I woke, David was still beside me but was sitting up. I rolled over and put my arm around his waist. "Is everything okay?" I asked.

He shifted down so we were face-to-face. "Okay? No. Blissful? Yes."

My cheeks flushed, and I rolled my eyes. "I'm the one in a state of bliss."

He brushed my lips with his. "We both are."

"Do you really mean that?"

"Of course I do. Why would you think otherwise?"

"You are clearly very good at sex while I, on the other hand…"

"Not sex, Sullivan. Making love, and I wouldn't say it's something I'm good at as much as it is that good between us."

"I think that is the most romantic thing I've ever heard."

"Get used to it." He nuzzled my neck. "I've got a million of them."

"That tickles," I said, giggling when he ran his tongue from my shoulder to beneath my ear.

"Are you hungry?"

"Starved."

"Let's eat the food my boss so kindly stocked for us."

After finishing the meal we prepared from the things Typhon had arranged to be delivered, we cleaned up, then sat in the living room, in front of the fireplace.

"It doesn't seem right to flip a switch and a roaring fire suddenly appears."

I chuckled. "I'd hardly call that roaring."

"Right. I'm not sure it even wards off the chill."

"We can keep each other warm," I said, snuggling closer.

David put his arms around me, but his body felt tense. "I like that idea."

"What's bothering you? Apart from the obvious."

"At some point, we need to address what's on the microSD card."

I nodded. "Can we wait until morning?"

I felt David nod too. "Of course. I'd rather wait longer, but there is some urgency in determining why Weber wants you dead." He squeezed tighter. "Sorry, I shouldn't have brought it up right before we return to bed."

"Let's talk about something else to get our minds off it."

"Brilliant plan. What about Christmas? What are some of your favorite memories?"

I had far more unpleasant ones of the holiday than otherwise, but I thought back to the last Christmas I remembered being fun. "My favorite was when your family still lived in Ballater."

"Yes, that was an enchanting time."

"Do you recall what we did?" I gazed up at him.

"I hadn't, but now that you mention it, I remember my father arranged for a sleigh ride on the grounds of Balmoral Castle, didn't he?"

"It was magical." If I closed my eyes, I could see it as though it was yesterday. "The royal family was there, not that we saw them. It was still exciting to think the Queen was in residence."

"My mum and I met her once. Lovely woman."

"We had hot chocolate with marshmallows your mum made."

"It was more likely Mrs. Drummond who arranged for us to have them, along with the Christmas meal we shared."

I laughed. "My mum was a dreadful cook, and I'll confess to not being any better. Having your parents host the meal was probably the last decent one we had."

"You did well enough tonight."

"All that was required was reheating. I'm quite adept at that."

"What about Christmases after that one?"

"They weren't much fun, honestly. My parents weren't social, except with yours, and as an only child, the day was quite lonely. Every day was. What about you? I imagine the holidays at Ashcroft Castle were brilliant."

"They were, but only because Con's and Tag's families spent the holidays with us. We actually rotated between our place, Blackmoor, and Glenshadow. The problem with that was on off years, Gus wasn't with us."

"Why not?"

"He was always invited, as was his mum, but she repeatedly declined, saying it wasn't proper for a housekeeper to spend the holidays with her employer."

"That's a shame."

"He never complained, but I would think it would be especially hard on Gus."

"The four of you are close."

"Very much so. They became my brothers. The same is true for them."

"Are you all only children?" I asked.

"Gus and I are. Con and Tag both have younger siblings. In Con's case, they're half-siblings."

"I suppose I could thank my parents for my boring home life since it's what inspired me to become a journalist."

"How so?" David asked.

"I devoured the newspaper. Every section, every article. It provided hours of entertainment back then. I remember how thick it was when it arrived. Now, it's hardly the size of a tabloid."

"The internet is to blame, I suppose."

"Sadly, it will likely lead to the demise of my profession."

David shook his head. "I disagree. There will always be a need for people like you who report on the Eric Webers of the world. How the news is delivered will continue to evolve. Like most things must." He turned to face me. "And here we are, back to all the things we shouldn't talk about before bed."

"We could stop talking altogether."

He grinned. "Yeah? And do what instead?"

"Kiss. Among other things."

I giggled when he scooped me off the sofa and carried me into the bedroom, where we spent most of the night doing those other things."

17

Savior

We spent two days at Typhon's flat in London before Con made contact, saying the security updates were complete at Ashcroft Castle and we could return.

While I was happy to leave the city, I would always remember his flat fondly, given it was where Sullivan and I had first made love. In fact, it was what we spent the majority of our time there doing.

In preparation for our departure, I requested Gus' help with several things. First, knowing that Sullivan had preferred staying in Primrose Croft over Glenshadow Castle or the flat, I asked him to ensure there'd be no security issues involved in our staying at Thistle Gate.

When he assured me it was as safe as anywhere else on the estate, I made my second request.

We traveled to Glasgow via the same private aircraft we'd flown on three days ago. Rather than by Condor, Angel was accompanied by Crash, whose call sign made Sullivan giggle. From the airfield, we had the same helicopter pilot ferry us, except rather than land at Glenshadow, we touched down on Ashcroft, where we were met by Gus.

"Welcome home," he said when we deboarded and raced over to the SUV.

"Couldn't have arranged warmer weather, mate?" I joked. It was well below zero this morning when the average temps could reach as high as twelve Celsius.

"My apologies. Next time."

I shuddered and put my arm around Sullivan. "I promise we're going someplace warm."

"Shall I—"

"Yes," I interrupted, wanting her to be surprised when we arrived at Thistle Gate.

"It all looks so beautiful," she commented on the ride from the open pasture through the woods and to where the view opened up to the castle. It, along with the surrounding grounds, had been decorated in a way I hadn't remembered since I was a child.

"You've gone all out," I commented to Gus.

"My mum's to thank, as always."

I chuckled, but it was true. Ashcroft had been her home since she was born, and while she'd always lived in quarters reserved for those in the family's employ, she took great pride in all of the estate looking its absolute best.

I felt a twinge of guilt that Mrs. Drummond was working at a time of year when she'd typically not be, but something told me getting to pull out all the stops for Sullivan made her happy.

When we passed Primrose Croft, I noticed Sullivan's disappointment and expected she'd ask where we were going. Perhaps the reason she hadn't was because we were already beyond the turnoff to the castle.

"This is Thistle Gate cottage," I said when Gus pulled the SUV up beside it. Like everywhere else, it was adorned with twinkling lights, greenery, and other Christmas decorations.

"It's so beautiful," Sullivan said when I came around, opened her door, and helped her out. "And it's right on the loch." She put her arm around me and kissed my cheek. "Thank you for bringing me here."

"If you're happy to, this is where we'll spend the majority of time. Or if you prefer the castle—"

"No. This is perfect. Unless you'd prefer—"

"I wouldn't."

Gus shook his head and chuckled at the way we kept interrupting each other. "Everything is as you wanted it," he said under his breath when he and I collected the bags from the back of the SUV.

"Including the locket?" I whispered.

"Yes, including that. You should also know Fallon is anxious to see Sullivan as soon as possible."

"Understood." Gus had informed me Ms. Wallace was staying at Blackmoor with Con, given the potential threat from Eric Weber. "How's it going with her and Infidel?"

"Neither has said. However, I wouldn't be surprised if the reason she's so anxious to see Sullivan is because she's had enough of Con."

"She could always stay at Shadowglen."

Gus nodded. "Or here."

Based on his smirk, he knew full well I wouldn't be in favor of that option.

"Shall we?" I asked, brushing past Sullivan on my way to the cottage's door.

She glanced up at the chimney, where smoke billowed. "A real fireplace," she murmured.

"More than one, in fact." As I went through the protocols to access the interior, I motioned to Gus. "Will Sullivan be able to come and go on her own?" I asked.

"I'll make sure of it before I leave."

"Many thanks," I said when the lock clicked and I opened the door.

Sullivan gasped when she followed me inside. "A Christmas tree?" Her eyes sparkled.

"And decorations," I said, motioning to the boxes containing ornaments I hadn't seen in years.

"My mum wanted me to give this to you," he said, standing between Sullivan and me with what looked like a journal in his hands. "With it, comes the message that this is only if you want to prepare some of your own meals. She and the staff are set up to fully provide whatever you'd like otherwise."

When my eyes met Sullivan's, we both laughed, then she held her hand out to take the book.

"Will she provide lessons?" she asked.

Gus grinned. "It would be her fondest Christmas memory to do so here in Thistle Gate."

"What a lovely name for it," Sullivan said, looking around the cottage that had never looked cozier.

"One I don't recall having heard before," I said. "Gus reminded me of it a few days ago."

"Only after my mum reminded me."

I took our bags to the largest of the three bedrooms while Gus gave Sullivan the rundown on the security systems recently installed, including setting up access.

"This is also for you," I said, walking over to the table where a mobile sat.

Before we left London, I asked Sullivan how she felt about not being with her parents for Christmas. She responded that she hadn't been for the last few years and it wasn't an issue. I'd already requested Gus arrange for her to have a secure mobile, but I especially wanted it to be here when we arrived after she said she did wish she could call them.

"If there's nothing else you need, I'll be on my way," said Gus. I'd already checked the kitchen and noted there was enough food prepared that the two of us wouldn't have to do our own cooking for several days, unless Sullivan decided she wanted to. I'd be happy either way. Truthfully, apart from needing sustenance, just being with her was all that mattered. Especially alone.

"Do the accommodations suit?" I asked when Gus stepped outside.

"It couldn't be nicer, David. I appreciate this more than you'll ever know."

"I hope you can feel somewhat at home here."

She laughed. "You'll regret those words should I truly make myself comfortable."

"Ah, yes, I recall you saying your flat was unorganized."

She raised a brow. "And that is being generous."

I squared my shoulders and raised my chin before gathering her in my arms. "I'm an SIS Sniper. I have no fear." We kissed in the same way we had been for the last couple of days. With passion and a complete lack of propriety, which I was reminded of when Gus opened the door and cleared his throat.

"Your mum's hot chocolate recipe," he said, handing me a thermos. It wasn't among the things I'd requested, but seeing the smile on Sullivan's face, I was very grateful he'd thought of it. Although it was more likely Mrs. Drummond who had.

"Many thanks," I repeated, escorting him to the door.

"Con is equally anxious to meet as Fallon is," he said quietly.

"Noted."

When I turned around, I saw Sullivan had removed her coat and was warming herself near the fireplace. "This couldn't be more ideal. Thank you," she said when I came up behind her and wrapped my arms around her waist.

"Can I interest you in hot chocolate?"

"I'd love it. May I?" She motioned to the boxes.

"By all means."

I poured two cups of cocoa and uncovered a plate I correctly guessed hid Christmas cookies, then carried all three into the living room.

When Sullivan held up an ornament, I saw her eyes were misty. "This is from your first Christmas."

I set the cups and plate on the table, then took it from her hand. It was a glass baby shoe, and written on the bottom was my date of birth, weight, and length. "Funny how it takes me back. I've forgotten so much about the time before my mum passed."

After Sullivan and I finished placing the ornaments and had devoured most of Mrs. Drummond's cookies, we made love in front of the fireplace. The glow of it and the lights on the tree on Sullivan's naked body made one of the most beautiful things I'd ever seen. Every minute I spent with her, I struggled not to confess my undying love for her. Instead, I lavished it on her with every touch of my hands, my mouth, and cock. With every special surprise I'd arranged and with every gaze when our eyes met. The best part was that I felt that love coming from her in the same way.

Despite wanting to use the excuse that it was Christmas Eve to beg off meeting with the guys and Fallon, I'd rather do it today than on Christmas.

When I broached the subject with Sullivan. She lamented the timing like I had, but concurred today would be preferable over tomorrow.

"How would you like to spend Christmas?" I asked, knowing a big gathering wouldn't be prudent from a security standpoint but that we might be able to have dinner with Gus and his mum at the castle.

"Am I terrible for saying I'd like to spend it alone with you?"

"Not at all," I responded, smiling broadly. "I had the same desire."

"Can we get the meeting over with, then?"

"As you wish." I sent a group message via the secure app we used and suggested gathering in my office, where we typically met, if everyone was agreeable. "They'll be here in one hour," I said when I received an immediate response.

"Then, we'd better hurry," she said, winking as she raced into the bedroom.

18

Sullivan

Rather than walk to the castle, David and I rode in the enclosed golf cart someone had left near Thistle Gate's front door.

I clutched my laptop bag, which contained the microSD card, close to my body. Today would be the first time I shared all its contents with anyone. Something I hadn't been able to imagine doing prior to now. That it was with David, Con, Tag, Gus, and Fallon, made it easier. They'd gained my trust, even in the short time I'd known them. David more so than the others.

My original plan was to share my findings with my uncle, Clive, given he was my immediate superior. Now, though, I couldn't imagine doing so. Not only had he lied about Fallon wanting to kill my investigation, but there was also a chance he'd conspired with Weber to kill *me*. When I shuddered, David reached over and took my hand.

"Are you all right?" he asked. "We don't have to do this now if you're not."

I shook my head. "I was just thinking about Clive."

He nodded. We'd talked about it a little while we were still at the flat in London, when he was sharing a story about his annoying uncle. I commented then that at least he didn't want David dead.

The first person we saw when we walked in the door of the castle was Mrs. Drummond.

"Thank you so much for all the lovely things you arranged at the cottage," I said, approaching her.

"It was a joy, my lady. I've precious memories of Thistle Gate." Her misty eyes were as curious to me as the statement. Had she spent much time here? Or maybe that's where she'd lived, and now, David and I had displaced her. I made a mental note to ask after the conclusion of our meeting.

"Come, they're waiting," he said after also thanking her with an affectionate embrace.

The four others were already in the room and immediately stood when David and I entered his office.

"Welcome back," said Fallon, walking over and taking both my hands in hers before we cheek-kissed.

"I'm happy to be," I said with sincerity before greeting Con, Tag, and Gus.

"I've asked Sullivan if she'd be willing to brief us on her investigation of Tower-Meridian, and she agreed." David turned to me. "Begin whenever you're ready."

"The entirety of what I've learned about the company, as well as about Eric Weber, is contained on this microSD card," I said, holding up the piece of cardboard where it was still affixed. "For now, I'll review it verbally, then at the conclusion of our meeting, I'll ask for copies to be made and distributed as necessary."

I began by recalling the night I'd first heard Eric Weber's name and how I'd overheard two men discussing him. "When one said he wouldn't dare show his face even after donating a billion dollars, I was intrigued. I suppose this is the perfect example of why curiosity kills the cat."

My eyes met David's, and in them, I saw such warmth. It—he—gave me the confidence to continue.

"While Tower-Meridian is well publicized for donations of that nature, along with their commitment to the distribution of humanitarian aid and medical supplies as well as emergency response services and refugee support, I believe it is all a smokescreen. What they really do is sinister at best, terrifying at worst."

Everyone in the room sat up straighter.

"Let's start with medical supplies…" I began as I had when I first told David about my investigation. "The arrival weights are significantly different from those taken at departure. This is also true of shipments containing humanitarian aid in the way of food supplies." I added that the difference was sometimes as much as thirty percent, and along with it, there were lost containers and suspicious and undocumented or traceable detours in shipment arrival. "The most obvious theory would be Tower-Meridian was selling the donated items on the black market."

"What led you to believe it was beyond that?" Fallon asked.

Again, I outlined the pieces of evidence like I had for David, saying that inventory reports on the manifests didn't match and the required temperature logs for sensitive medications were either incomplete or missing altogether.

"The biggest mystery was how a shipping company as large as this could experience communications blackouts as well as blocked satellite tracking." I pointed at the drive. "There are multiple documents detailing everything I've just told you."

"Where did you get this information? Who were your sources?" Con asked.

My eyes met Fallon's, and she shook her head.

"I'm not ready to divulge that information. I may never be."

Rather than anger, what I saw in Con's eyes was respect. His question had been a test that I'd passed.

"Explain about the two ports," David prompted.

"Right. Most larger UK shipping companies, of which Tower-Meridian is one of the biggest in existence, are registered in Felixstowe. Tees is the home port for every vessel I've identified as being theirs."

"If I may," said David.

"Go ahead."

"The working theory is that Weber is intentionally exploiting the inherent chaos in traveling between two such different ports." He looked over at me. "Right?"

I smiled. "Correct and close to verbatim what I said. And, as David alluded to, the manifests are signed off at Tees and spot-checked in Felixstowe."

"Where they're most likely getting rubber-stamped without anyone ever checking," said Tag.

"Correct."

"What do you think he's transporting?" Con asked.

"As I also told David, my first theory was he was heavy into human trafficking. Based on the communications blackouts alone, combined with blocked tracking, Tower-Meridian's ships could make any number of stops virtually anywhere in the world."

"And now?" Con pressed.

"Weapons are the next most obvious."

I caught a look between him and David.

"Except that isn't enough," Con muttered. "The risk they're taking is disproportionate to either form of trafficking."

"As David said the other day, a series of well-timed raids would bury them," I added.

Con nodded. "Which means whatever it is they're moving isn't discernible or at least not immediately obvious." His eyes met mine. "So what is it?"

"I don't know," I admitted.

"Do you have a guess?" Fallon asked.

Had anyone else posed the same question, I would've responded, in my line of work, I couldn't afford to guess. Fallon too would've given the same stock answer.

"Something far worse, obviously, but what? I can't fathom."

"You're right about whatever it is being far worse. The problem as it stands right now is Weber believes you've figured it out. And if you haven't, you're close enough that he sees you as a big-enough threat that he'll take you out regardless of risk," said Con.

"What do you think it is?" Fallon asked him.

"Weapons of mass destruction would make sense, but how would he get his hands on them, in the first place, let alone load them into containers? The payoffs at the ports would be staggering, plus with that number of people, the odds of discovery are astronomical," I responded.

"Except you also believe that whatever it is, isn't discernible. WMDs certainly would be, unless what he's moving is something no one has ever seen before," said Gus.

My eyes met Fallon's. That was exactly right. And if no one had seen whatever it was before, how could it ever be detected?

"Where do we go from here?" Tag asked.

"Let's take a look at the UK's biggest enemies. Not just ours, but the rest of the world's," said Con.

"Russia and China," Fallon responded. "And in China's case, they see the US as the biggest threat. Not that they're alone in that opinion."

"But collectively, Russia and China are neck and neck," said David.

"So the next step is to dig deeper into who Tower-Meridian would most likely partner with," said Con.

"Both," I responded.

Con and Fallon nodded.

"Right," she muttered.

"Well, Happy Christmas, one and all," said Tag, pushing back his chair. "And before you apologize, my guess is you didn't want to do this today any more than the rest of us did," he said to me.

"I did not. However, I personally don't believe we have the luxury of burying our heads in the sand any longer."

Everyone in the room murmured their agreement.

"Before we break for the afternoon, can we talk about tomorrow?" Con asked. "Given the security risks inherent with a large gathering, I propose those of us here presently celebrate together."

I looked to David, who appeared to be surveying the room and noticing, that like I had, everyone seemed to be in agreement.

"I'd not ask to take you away from your families," I said.

"The reality is, Sullivan, that everyone here is in a great deal of danger. I'd suggest we all consider that spending time with anyone outside of our small group puts those we come in contact with in peril," said Con.

"Understood."

I walked over to the window and looked out at the loch while David spoke with the other men.

"I'm proud of you," said Fallon, coming to stand beside me. "I hope you don't mind my saying so."

"Not at all. It's an honor."

"You and I have much to discuss, but it can wait a couple more days."

"Such as?"

She leaned closer. "What I found in both Glenshadow's and Blackmoor's libraries and what I believe might be in the ones here. Also, Clive Edwards. We've been keeping tabs on him while, at the same time, taking a deeper look at his financials of the last few months."

My stomach clenched. "Oh God," I groaned.

"I'm sorry, Sullivan."

"Don't be. Whatever my uncle has gotten himself involved in is his doing. Not yours or mine."

"I agree. I'll add that finding out one's relative might be linked to the very man you're investigating as part of the job where he serves as your superior can be disconcerting."

"Thinking he had something to do with someone trying to kill me is far worse."

She put her hand on my arm. "I'm glad we'll be spending part of Christmas together."

"As am I." We embraced when Con asked if she was ready to leave.

I hung back when David walked them out, as did Gus.

"How are you holding up?" he asked.

"Better than I was when I was mostly alone in all this. When you don't have anyone else's feedback or input, it's easy to think it's all too far-fetched."

"Now, you know it isn't."

"Listen, I know this is asking next to the impossible, but I was wondering if you might be able to help me with something."

"Anything."

I smiled. "There's something I want to give to David tomorrow."

He raised a brow. "How far to the ends of the earth must I travel to get it?"

"Not far at all."

"Then, consider it done."

I quickly explained what I wanted when I saw David on his way inside.

"On my way," Gus said, winking.

"I don't know about you, but I am ready for it to just be you and me back at the cottage."

"Sounds perfect." I looked around the room we were in. "What was it like growing up in a castle?"

"Surprisingly ordinary. It's my belief that regardless of the size of one's home, there are only certain rooms where we spend the majority of our time. If I were to really think about it, I doubt it would be more than the total number in Thistle Gate." He touched the tip of my nose with his finger. "You, on the other hand, would have to explore every nook and cranny of each and every one in this place."

"How many are there?"

"Can you believe I've no idea?"

"Mrs. Drummond would."

"Let's ask her tomorrow."

I smiled, put my arms around his neck, and kissed him. "Sounds perfect."

He put his arms around my waist and nuzzled my neck. "God, I love you."

I felt David freeze. I wasn't sure he was even breathing. I leaned away far enough to see his face, but he wouldn't look at me.

"Forgive me," he whispered.

I put my hand on his cheek. "Are you apologizing for saying the words to me I've dreamed you would someday?"

His eyes were misty when they met mine. "It was too soon."

I shook my head. "It's taken you twenty years."

When he smiled, I kissed him, then took his hand.

"Let's go home."

"I cannot tell you how good that sounds."

19

Savior

I pushed away every ounce of disappointment I felt over Sullivan not telling me she loved me too. I hadn't planned to blurt it out the way I had, and it wasn't fair that I'd expect her to say it back after being together a few short days.

I did love her, though, like I knew I'd never love another. If by fate, she and I parted ways one day, the Ashcroft line would die with me, and I was okay with that. What I couldn't do was be with any other woman, raise a family with any other woman. Yes, it was crazy that I fell in love with her when we were children. It didn't make it any less real.

The drive to the cottage was as silent as it could be, given we were in an ancient golf cart. Had we wanted to talk, we wouldn't have been able to hear one another anyway.

"I don't know about you, but I could stand to eat something more substantial than Christmas cookies,"

I said once we were inside the cottage, warming ourselves by the fire.

"We could eat," she said, her eyes smiling as much
as her lips.

"Or?"

Sullivan took my hand, then led me into the bedroom and over to the bed, where she pushed me until I
sat on the edge. Starting with my shirt, she removed all
my clothes, then stepped back and removed her own.

Once we were both naked, she moved the bedclothes
out of our way and lay down, pulling me with her.

Since she didn't speak, I didn't either. Instead, I
remained still as she ran her hands and mouth over the
entirety of my body. When I moved my arm once, she
shook her head.

After taking me in her mouth and refusing to stop
even when I told her I was about to come, Sullivan
kissed her way up my torso, stopping at my heart to
rest her hand and bringing mine up to cover hers. Then
she looked up at me.

"I believe we've owned each other's hearts since the
moment we met. How else could you have possibly
recognized a woman you hadn't seen since she was

a little girl, unless something in your soul whispered you'd finally found your other half, something we both believed might never be?"

"I—"

Sullivan put her finger on my lips. "I love you, David."

My restraint snapped, and I rolled our bodies so I was on top of her, wanting to kiss every inch of her like she'd done to me, but I needed it all at once. I settled on her lips, my tongue twining with hers between repeatedly telling her I loved her. At some point, I realized it wasn't my voice alone. She said it back as often as I did.

After making love again more times than I could count, Sullivan and I foraged for food in the kitchen, then sat by the light of the tree, snuggling in front of the fireplace.

"It's hard to believe that the scariest night of my life had led to me being happier than I ever imagined possible."

I kissed her temple. "I cannot tell you how many times I've thanked God, a higher power, or the universe that it was me who Typhon sent that night. That I was close enough to be first on the scene."

She shuddered.

"Sorry. I was, and we're here, and that's all that matters."

Sullivan rested her head on my chest. "I've wondered too if maybe it's why we're both loners. Or we were. What if you found someone else? What if I did?"

"Remember, my love, I'm the best sniper SIS has ever had. Sadly, you might've been a widow until you found your way to me."

She giggled. "It's *awful* that I find that funny."

I shrugged. "No one here to judge us."

When she yawned, I took her plate to the kitchen, then scooped her up and returned to the bedroom with her in my arms.

"Father Christmas will not come unless we're asleep before midnight," I said, holding her close.

"He wouldn't get here at all with the amount of security roaming around, not to mention that which can't be seen."

"You weren't meant to see any of it. Or them. I suppose thinking you wouldn't notice was naive on my part."

"David, wake up! It's snowing," said Sullivan, jostling me.

"You're dreaming, my love. It rarely snows in this part of Scotland."

She tugged on my arm until I opened my eyes and looked out the window, where, just as she'd said, snow was falling.

"It's perfect."

"Wait, where are you going?" I asked when she ran out of the room, wearing a robe I didn't know was here or who it belonged to.

"I have to check on something. Stay where you are."

I heard a clap, then felt her when she tumbled back in bed, then crawled on top of me. "Happy Christmas, David."

"Happy Christmas, Sullivan."

"Turns out I was wrong about St. Nicholas."

I raised my head. "What do you mean?"

"Apparently, I underestimated his ability to circumvent security."

I shook my head and chuckled. "Are you saying he delivered gifts?"

Her eyes opened wide, and she nodded slowly.

"This, I have to see. By the way, where did you get the robe?"

"I found it hanging on a hook inside the closet. Would you like me to get yours?"

"I wasn't aware I had one."

"You do." She pointed to her robe. "Look, it even has our names embroidered."

I blinked a couple of times, and sure enough, I noticed the one she wore said Sullivan.

"I think Mrs. Drummond is the real Santa Claus."

She nodded. "I believe you might be right."

My eyes opened wide, and my mouth gaped when I saw the number of gifts under the tree that, last night, was empty. "When and who?" I muttered.

"While you were still sleeping, and Gus."

"Ah, how kind but also unnecessary."

Sullivan shrugged. "Just kind, I think." She pulled her hand from behind her back. In her palm, sat a small, perfectly wrapped box. "He had to deliver this. It's for you."

"Hang on." I went around her and grabbed a similarly sized box that I'd hidden yesterday before we left for the meeting at the castle. I held it out. "And this is for you."

"Let's sit."

I followed her to the sofa, and we exchanged the presents.

"Go ahead. Open yours first," I said.

She untied the ribbon, tossed it to the side, then tore open the paper. "What is it?" she asked, running her finger over the antique box her gift was in.

"Open it and find out."

She gasped at the sight of the locket that had belonged to my mum and that Gus had arranged to have cleaned and brought to me.

"It's so beautiful." She gingerly removed it from its container. "Is there anything inside?"

"Take a look."

She gasped again and covered her mouth with her hand. "Where did you get this?" she asked, pointing to the photo of her when she was eight.

"Turns out Mrs. Drummond remembered seeing one in an old photo album."

Sullivan raised a brow.

"She did. I swear it."

"This is the Davy I remember," she said, staring at the photo on the locket's opposite side.

"I wish it wasn't."

"You were adorable."

I raised a brow. "*You* were the adorable one."

"Open your gift."

I carefully untied the ribbon, then lifted each place the paper had been taped. Between each flap, I looked up at her.

"You're doing this on purpose, aren't you?"

"What?" I asked, making a point of looking down at the wrapping she'd dropped on the floor.

I lifted the hinged cover and found a silver pocket watch inside.

Sullivan leaned forward. "Open it."

Under the cover was an inscription. "For all our moments together," I read aloud before bringing it closer to my eyes. "Is that an A?"

"Yes, 'to A from A,'" she said. "I didn't notice the initials when I first saw it. I just liked the inscription."

"I love it, Sullivan. When did you…you know?"

"I saw it several days ago in a newspaper circular from an antique store and couldn't stop thinking about it. Blessed Gus contacted them for me, and they still had it. He somehow managed to get it here by this morning. Quite the miracle worker, he is."

"The same for me," I said, pointing to the locket.

"He's a good man, David."

I nodded. "The best, and while I'm close to Con and Tag, it's Gus who's always been like a real brother."

I remembered the photo on the shelf in my grandfather's study, hoping it was still there so I could show it to her.

"Would you like to wear the locket?"

"I would—every day for the rest of my life."

After fastening the clasp around her neck, I kissed her. "I love you."

"And I love you. Oh, and before I forget, I invited Gus and his mum to have breakfast with us."

"And they agreed?" I was stunned.

"Yes, and according to him, his mother cried when he told her."

"I hope she doesn't again when she finds out what abysmal cooks we both are."

"About that." Sullivan got up and went into the kitchen. "She planned ahead and made something I only have to pop in the oven, which I'm sure I could handle if I could figure out how to turn the bloody thing on."

"Let me see." It took me close to five minutes to finally manage it, only seconds before I was about to call Gus to ask. "What time will they be here?"

"An hour, which is how long she said this should be in the oven."

"Then, we'd better hurry," I said, winking as we raced into the bedroom.

20

Sullivan

In an effort to save time, David and I made love in the shower. To think I'd gone from a woman who'd had sex exactly once in her life and wondered what the fuss was about, given the disappointing experience, to one that craved intimacy every waking moment was astounding.

More astonishing was how I wanted to be with David all the time. I'd often wondered, if I did have a boyfriend, if I'd be able to stand his presence more than a few hours a week.

"I'd love to know what you're thinking," David said when I pulled the dish that Mrs. Drummond had so kindly prepared for us from the oven.

"How I'm sure you'll soon be sick of spending time with me."

He cocked his head, but before he could ask anything more, there was a knock at the door.

"Come in. Happy Christmas," he said, kissing Mrs. Drummond's cheek and putting his hand on Gus' shoulder. The three seemed more like a family than employee, coworker, and duke. I wondered if he realized it.

Thinking about family reminded me I should contact my parents today. I dreaded the stilted, affected conversation, particularly on holidays. My mum would complain about something, usually having to do with me. My father would mutter his hellos and get off the phone as quickly as he could.

I glanced up from where I'd set plates on the counter, along with the bowl of fruit Mrs. Drummond had also prepared. While her back was to the men, I could see her face clearly. Tears streaked down her cheeks as she looked around the festive room.

"Happy Christmas," I said, walking over and squeezing her hand.

She quickly wiped the tears away and smiled. "It warms my heart to see Thistle Gate this way. It's been years…" Her voice trailed off, and she flushed as though she hadn't meant to add the last part.

"Did you spend much time here?" I asked.

"None at all."

Her words, combined with the way she held her hands at her sides, barely moving otherwise, and her seeming inability to meet my eyes, told me she was lying.

"I feared David and I were keeping you from your home when we decided to stay here rather than at the smaller cottage or the castle."

She brought her hand to her cheek. "The castle has always been my home."

While I'd comment on how nice that must be, no doubt the part she lived in was considered servants' quarters—regardless of how archaic the term was these days.

"Always? Have you lived here all your life?"

Over her shoulder, I noticed both David and Gus listening to the conversation rather than engaging in one of their own.

"My mother, Agnes, was housekeeper here when I was a wean."

"What of your father?"

She fidgeted and glanced behind her. "Look at me, monopolizing the conversation when it was so very kind of you to invite Angus and me to join you."

"It was our pleasure," David said, walking over to stand beside us.

"Not to mention, we have you to thank for our breakfast." I motioned to the dishes I'd arranged on the counter. "Shall we dine at the table?"

"I'll help," David offered, meeting me in the kitchen. He leaned closer and kissed my cheek. "Thank you for doing this. I'm ashamed to say it wouldn't have occurred to me."

"She's clearly touched to be here."

He glanced over at her. "Which makes me feel even worse."

I'd say there was more to it, but as it was only con-jecture, I held my tongue.

While we ate, David and Gus reminisced about Christmases past, mostly from their childhoods. The stories they told had me giggling to the point of tears.

"May I get you anything else, Mrs. Drummond?" I asked when I noticed her empty plate.

"Mairi, please, dear. And no, I'm quite full, thank you."

Her gaze traveled from my eyes to the locket. As though my arm had a will of its own, I reached up and fingered it.

"David arranged for Father Christmas to have this delivered this morning," I said, winking at Gus.

"That's not all he brought," said David, pulling the watch from his trouser pocket and holding it out for them to see. "It has an inscription that reads, 'For all our moments together.'" He reached over and took my hand, and I beamed.

"Mum, are you all right?" Gus asked.

I glanced over at her wide-eyed expression and pale face. "Yes, fine." Her gaze remained focused on David's gift. "Wherever did…?" Her voice trailed off like it had earlier.

"I saw it in an advertisement what seems like weeks ago. Your son was gracious enough to secure it for me, thus earning him the Father Christmas moniker."

"It's lovely. May I take a closer look?"

"Of course," said David, handing it to her.

She studied the inscription.

"I've no idea who A and A are. The photo I saw of it wasn't detailed enough for me to notice."

She nodded but didn't raise her eyes. "It's quite old, but still works," she mumbled.

David's eyes met mine, then we both looked over at Gus.

"Have you seen the watch before, Mum?" he asked.

Her expression changed from reminiscent to startled. "Of course I haven't," she said, plastering what looked like a fake smile on her face.

"It seems you recognize it," he pressed.

"I've seen one similar, is all." She returned it to David. "It's a lovely gift. They both are."

"The locket was my mum's," he said. "But you already know that, given you found the photo of Sullivan."

While she smiled, something about the watch appeared to have rattled her.

I fingered the locket. "I love it, and I never intend to take it off."

"I see there are more gifts beneath the tree," said Gus.

"You would take note of that," David teased. "Are there any with your name?"

"Let's go look, shall we?" I said, pushing away from the table. "Oh no, leave that right where it is," I scolded when Mrs. Drummond picked up her plate.

"I'm happy to help."

I put my hand on her arm. "And I'm happier to have you as our guest."

Her eyes filled with tears she quickly blinked away. "I'm honored, my lady."

"Tsk, tsk, Mairi. As I've said, please call me Sullivan." I waved my finger, and she smiled.

"Your grandfather would be so pleased to see it this way," I heard her say to David.

"Speaking of him," he left the room and returned a few seconds later, carrying a framed photo. "I saw this the other day." He handed it to her.

"Ah, look at you wee lads," said Mairi, running her finger over the frame. "'Twas a favorite of his."

David looked over at me with a puzzled expression that mirrored my own. Even Gus appeared confused.

"Would you like to have it?" David asked.

"Oh no, I couldn't," she said, handing it back to him.

"Please. I'd like you to," he said, keeping his hands at his sides.

"That's very kind, but—"

"It's a gift, Mum. Say thank you."

Her cheeks flushed at her son's admonishment, but she clutched the frame to her chest.

After we opened the gifts beneath the tree, Gus and Mairi thanked us again and bid their goodbyes.

"Is it me, or were her reactions odd?" David asked after closing the door behind them.

"I was going to say the same thing."

"Perhaps it's the holidays. We haven't celebrated them here, at Ashcroft, in years. I typically relieve the staff from their duties the final two weeks of the year, along with the first week of the new year. I asked Gus to inform his mother I didn't expect her to work this year, but he insisted she'd want to. I should've spoken to her directly."

"I'm sure he was right in saying she'd want to be here."

"She seemed so sad. It was nearly heartbreaking."

I shook my head. "I don't think it was sad as much as nostalgic. Were she and your grandfather close?"

"Close?" He cringed. "No offense to her, but Angus—who I never called Grandfather, by the way—was from a bygone era where the duke and the housekeeper didn't interact."

My mouth gaped. "Angus?"

"I know what you're thinking, but it was Gus' father's name."

"A and A," I said under my breath.

He raised a brow.

"You're about to say I should've considered a career in fiction writing, aren't you?"

He smiled. "My apologies for saying that to you before."

"It wasn't at all nice."

"How can I make it up to you?" He wrapped his arms around me.

"I have a few ideas. However, first, I must call my parents." I grimaced.

"We could've figured out a way to visit—"

I appreciated the offer. "As much as I'm not looking forward to a phone call, spending the day with them would've been worse. I should just get it over with."

"Shall I give you some privacy?"

"I'd rather you not." I looked around the room, then in the direction of the kitchen. "I don't suppose there are any spirits stocked in the cottage."

"I'm sure there are. What do you fancy?" he asked, winking.

"I was kidding."

David put his hand on my cheek. "You weren't."

I nodded. "You're right. A shot of anything would probably take the edge off."

He walked down the hallway and returned with a decanter and two glasses. "Angus' favorite brandy."

"How long ago did he pass?"

David laughed. "The decanter was empty the last I noticed, so it's safe to say either Mrs. Drummond or Gus filled it."

"Thanks," I said when he handed me the glass he'd poured. "Here goes," I added after I'd downed it.

"Hello?" my mum answered.

"Happy Christmas," I said, doing my best to sound sincere.

"*Sullivan?* Where in heaven's name are you?"

"What do you mean? When last we spoke, I informed you I wouldn't be coming this year." Or any other year, I thought to myself.

"We've been worried sick. Your uncle is here. Hang on, he wants to speak with you."

"Wait, Mum!"

"Sullivan, we've been trying to reach you," Clive repeated. "Quite urgently, in fact."

David was seated close enough to hear both sides of the conversation and reached out to take my free hand. "Have you? What ever for?"

"Have you forgotten who you work for?"

Both David and I raised a brow.

"Not any more than I've forgotten that I, along with most of the rest of the staff, am on holiday."

"It's imperative we meet. Immediately."

"That won't be possible."

"Where are you? I'll come to you."

Where? I mouthed to David.

"The States," he responded when I hit the mobile's mute button.

"Right. Perfect." I tapped the button again. "We can get together after the holiday, Clive. I'll be in town after the first of the year, like always."

"I said we need to meet immediately. I did not say after the first of the year. If you value your job—"

"It's a nine-hour flight from the States," I blurted, fearing my temper wouldn't hold much longer.

"What are you doing in America?"

"As I've said repeatedly, I'm on holiday. Would you please put my mother back on the line?"

"I'm not finished. I expect you to be on the next flight. Let me know the details."

I bit my tongue. "My mum, please."

"I'll warn you, if you don't do as I say, you'll be terminated from your position with the Crown Herald."

"Terminated. Interesting word choice," I mumbled.

"What was that?"

"I asked to speak with my mother. Or my father. Either one."

"Sullivan, please do as your uncle asks," my mother said when he handed the phone back to her.

"Happy Christmas, Mum. Please give my regards to Dad."

I hit end on the call, dropped the mobile, and put my head in my hands. "My God," I muttered.

David tried to pull me into his arms, but I stiffened. "We should speak with Fallon."

How I loved him for saying we should rather than I should. His support meant everything to me. I didn't realize how alone I'd been before. "Thank you," I said, looking into his eyes.

"They're scheduled to arrive this afternoon. However, I think it would be best if I contacted Con and asked them to come earlier."

My eyes filled with tears.

"But first, allow me to hold you."

I fell against him as tears poured from my eyes. He stroked my hair, soothing me as I sobbed.

"I love you, Sullivan," he said more than once.

My self-pity rose to the surface, and the flow of my tears increased as all I could think was how thankful I was that someone did.

After he held me for several minutes and my tears subsided, I sat up. "Thank you."

"Thank *you*," he responded.

I shook my head and smiled. "You are a savior—mine, in fact."

He leaned forward and kissed me. "I'm not being trite when I say you're mine too." He reached for his mobile. "I'll ring Con now."

21

Savior

"Apologies for interrupting Christmas with this," I began when Sullivan, Gus, and I gathered in my office in the castle with Fallon, Con, and Tag. "When Sullivan contacted her parents today, she learned Clive Edwards was at their home." He looked over at me. "Do you want to recount the conversation, or shall I?"

"I can do it." She took a deep breath. "While much more than this was said, Clive threatened my job unless I agreed to meet with him."

"How did the conversation end?" Fallon asked.

"I may have led him to believe I was in the States." Both women smiled.

"Con, have you been able to find anything connecting him and Weber?" I asked.

"Not directly. However, your instincts about his finances were spot on. The man has been living well beyond his means. It also appears he has heavy gambling debts."

"Mobile records?"

"Several calls made to numbers indicative of burner phones. None more than once."

"What about that night?" Sullivan asked. No one needed her to say which she spoke of.

"There was one at seventeen hundred hours," Con responded.

"I'm unsure what steps to take," said Fallon.

"Anything done now will tip him off and likely Weber too," said Tag.

"Speaking of Weber."

When Con hesitated, I knew it was something I wasn't going to like. "Go on," I snapped.

"He has diplomatic protection."

"*What?* From whom?"

"Syria. And, yes, I have verified that he holds dual citizenship," Con added.

"A Russian ally."

"China's as well," Fallon added.

"As I said the other day," Con began. "Whoever he has working for him has been able to bury most everything about the man. My best estimation is that one parent was from the UK and the other Syrian."

"What does this mean in terms of prosecution?" I asked.

"Unlikely."

Then, he had to die. It was as simple as that. I'd address the possibility with Typhon tomorrow.

"Clearly, the only option is assassination," Tag muttered from where he stood near the window.

My eyes met his. "I wouldn't have said it," I muttered.

While I expected him to give me some kind of grief, he didn't. "I know," was his only comeback.

"What of Clive Edwards?" Fallon asked. "It'll be easy enough to put him off until after the holiday break, particularly since I'm also in the States." She winked at Sullivan.

"His desperation will cause him to screw up," said Con.

"I could confront him."

All eyes turned to Sullivan.

"Absolutely not," I said in too loud a voice.

She raised her chin in my direction. Clearly, that wasn't the right thing to say, given the look on her face. I couldn't think of any way to backpedal, however.

"I'd like to suggest we split into smaller groups, each with a specific mandate. Sullivan and I will work together," said Fallon. "There's something major at play here that we're not seeing, and spinning our wheels is getting us nowhere."

"I have a contact in Syria," offered Tag. I was stunned but wouldn't ask who or why.

"I'll continue working on the encrypted communications," said Con. "There's got to be at least a few I can crack open."

"Is there a library?" Fallon asked.

"Of course. I'll lead the way," I offered, hoping to be able to speak to Sullivan alone.

"A moment, sir?" Mrs. Drummond asked.

"Err, certainly," I responded when Sullivan scowled at me. "The library is just ahead on the right." I watched them walk away, silently willing her to look over her shoulder at me. She didn't.

"What is it?" I asked, snapping at the last person who deserved it. "Apologies, Mairi. What can I assist with?"

"I was wondering how you'd like to handle Christmas dinner."

"I have no preference."

She leaned closer. "What I mean to say is, what about Ambrose?"

"Bloody hell," I said under my breath. "I'd forgotten he was here."

"Would there be an issue with him joining you?"

Beyond annoyance? Probably not. Sullivan's presence on the estate was hardly a secret at this point. "Please issue the invitation. There's always the chance he'll decline."

"Unlikely, and yes, sir."

It was on the tip of my tongue to ask about her earlier behavior at Thistle Gate, except what would I say? Not to mention, Sullivan was quite miffed at me presently.

When I approached the library, I found her sitting on her own, studying her computer. "May I interrupt?"

"Yes." She barely glanced in my direction, even when I took the seat next to her.

"I overstepped and I apologize." I ran my finger down her arm.

Her gaze met mine. "Why did you?"

"Protecting you has become a reflex. I know that's a horrible excuse, but…"

"Go on."

I scooted closer. "If anything should happen to you, I don't know how I'd bear it." My words were hardly above a whisper, but I was close enough for her to hear me.

"He's my uncle. It should be my decision."

"I agree and will offer my apologies a second time."

"Accepted."

"Am I forgiven?"

"Yes," she said, looking up when Fallon entered the room.

"Sorry to interrupt."

When Sullivan told her she wasn't, I took that as my cue to leave. "We'll speak later?" I asked.

"Of course."

"Well, I made a bloody mess of that," I said, rejoining Con and Gus.

"I'd say," Gus muttered.

"By the way, your mum stopped me on the way to the library to inquire about Brose joining us for dinner."

"I hope you said no," said Con before looking up at me. "You didn't, did you?"

"It's Christmas."

Con nodded. "Please do not seat him next to me."

"I doubt there will be a seating chart. So, did Tag leave?"

"He said he'd be back later," Gus responded.

"I can't help but wonder who he knows in Syria."

"Nightingale," said Con.

"Come again?"

"Leila Nassar. Like we suspect with Weber, she holds dual citizenship and was recruited some time ago by SIS. She's currently undercover in Damascus."

"I've not heard of her."

Con and Gus looked at each other and laughed.

"What?"

"It isn't as though you pay attention to that sort of thing."

"That sort of thing?"

"You're more of an assignment guy. It's what makes you so good. You're focused," Con continued.

"I hardly need you to blow smoke up my arse."

He chuckled again. "And what if I said I'd contacted Typhon about sniper training?"

"Fair point. So, what you're saying is, when it comes to investigative work, I'm no help?"

My two friends made eye contact again.

"Give me *something* to do."

"Tag might need your help when he returns."

I wasn't welcome with Sullivan and Fallon and wasn't needed here. Rather than continue to interrupt Con and Gus, who appeared quite focused, I got up and left the room.

When I saw Brose crossing the bridge, heading in the direction of Thistle Gate, I rushed out and called his name.

"Ah, Ash, I was hoping for a word," he said when I caught up with him.

"What about?"

"There appears to be a great deal going on around here. Thistle Gate, in particular."

"Interestingly, I wasn't aware of the cottage's name until recently."

"My father was quite enamored with the place. For good reason, I'd say."

"What would that be?" I asked.

"Surely, you know."

I stopped walking. "Know what, Brose?"

"About your grandfather and the housekeeper. What was her name?"

"Agnes MacDonald?"

He pointed at me. "That's it. Angus and Agnes. The least well-kept secret in the west of Scotland."

"I had no idea," I murmured, replaying Mrs. Drummond's odd behavior this morning. Wait. *Mrs. Drummond.* "Good Lord," I said under my breath. Could it be?

Brose chuckled. "You've finally pieced it together, eh?"

"I need a drink. Join me?" I said when we reached the gate that led to the cottage's entrance—the one I hadn't noticed had thistles woven into the design. Con and Gus were certainly right about my lack of investigative skills. It was a wonder I could locate my own nose.

"I'm anxious to see what you've done with the place."

Once inside, his eyes opened wide. "I never took you for someone who celebrates the holiday."

"I've a reason to this year." I poured two glasses of brandy and handed him one. "Cheers."

"Cheers," he repeated. "The young lady inspired all this?"

"Yes."

"You remind me of your father when he met Alexandria. Same lovesick expression."

"Yeah? What about you, Brose? You've never brought a woman around. Why is that?"

"I did once, many years ago."

"It's a day for stories I've never been told. Who was she?"

My uncle's expression darkened to the point where I regretted asking.

"Sorry. I didn't mean to pry."

He took a hefty pull from his glass and held it out for more. "No one would've told you, would they have?"

"I'm not following," I said, giving him a little extra.

"How do you think your parents met?"

I was stunned. "*No.* Through you?"

"Your mother was the only woman I ever loved. Not that she ever knew."

"Did you say you brought her to Ashcroft?"

"Aye. We were friends at university, and I invited her for the weekend. I suppose I was showing off a bit."

"Did my father know how you felt about her?"

He shook his head. "No one did. Until now."

"God, Brose. I don't know what to say. I'm sorry."

"That was a long time ago. Over thirty years. Admittedly, my heart broke in pieces back then. I eventually got over it."

I thought back to him spending time here while my dad was still alive. I didn't recall it being often.

"I went a bit off the rails, as they say. Drank too much. Blew through the measly stipend your father allowed."

I bristled, not wanting to hear this part.

"Anyway. The Lord took your mother far too young. Your father too."

"Gus reminded me that my grandfather was the only one to live much beyond his fifties. And you, of course."

My eyes opened wide, and Brose nodded.

"Wait. Are you suggesting he was also Gus' grandfather? My God, of course he was." I shook my head. "I had no idea. Truly."

"That's the way he wanted it. I always felt bad for Mairi. And Agnes, of course. Living their life in secret. We had quite a row about it, in fact."

"You and grandfather?" I recalled telling Sullivan earlier I'd never called him that.

"He was livid with me. Rightly so, I suppose."

I poured more brandy for each of us and rested against the sofa. I'd avoided my uncle for most of my life, mainly because my father rarely had a kind word to say about him. Now, I felt terrible for it.

"I owe you an apology."

He shook his head. "You do not. I deserved their ire."

"Your brother stole your girlfriend, and your father had a child out of wedlock that he wouldn't acknowledge. I'd say whatever your behavior was, was justified."

"I tried to blackmail him."

I'd just taken a drink and nearly spit it out. "Grandfather?"

Brose nodded. "That was the reason he was so angry with me. Tossed me out, in fact."

"I'm sorry, Brose."

"Again, it was my fault. We never spoke again." I looked away when he teared up. How many times could I repeat how sorry I was to hear about a life I'd never given much thought to until now?

"There's something I want to show you." I dug in my pocket for the watch. "What do you know about this?"

I handed it to him, and when he opened it and read the inscription, he looked as though he might lose the contents of his stomach. *"Where did you get this?"*

I was astonished he'd raised his voice. "It was a gift from Sullivan. The, err, woman you've seen about. She said she saw it in an antique dealer's advertisement."

"I'll be damned," he said under his breath.

"Apparently, you've seen it before. Mrs. Drummond, err, Mairi had a similar reaction."

Brose's gaze remained fixated on the watch. "I took it."

"Come again?"

A tear ran down his cheek. "You heard me."

"And sold it?"

"Nah, it wasn't worth anything, except sentimentally. That's why I did it."

I wanted to ask how it wound up in the hands of an antique dealer, but that wasn't important now.

"I've treated you terribly, Ambrose, and I'm truly sorry for that."

He finished what was in his glass. "I appreciate the sentiment, Ash, but I'm not worthy of it." He stood. "I'll take my leave now. Thank you for the drink."

"Must you go? You'll join us for dinner later, yes?"

He shook his head. "I think not." When he walked out, I wanted to run after him. I still had so many questions, but that was hardly fair to him. I'd avoided conversing with the man most of my life, and now, I only wanted to in order to get information out of him.

Sullivan

"He meant well," Fallon said when David left us on our own.

"I'm unaccustomed to being shut down that way. In fact, it's reminiscent of both my mother and her brother."

"Clive?"

I nodded. "My dear uncle Clive."

"The situation with him is problematic."

I laughed. "Problematic?"

She laughed too. "Apologies. It is far worse than that."

"I'd say," I muttered.

"You may not want to hear this, but I agree with Ash about not confronting him. Better to see what he does next. There's a good chance he'll lead us to Weber."

"You're right." I looked up at her. "I never liked him. Even before I thought he set me up to be assassinated. Is that what they'd call it?" I lowered my voice an octave. "'Breaking news this evening. An unidentified female was assassinated outside Edinburgh Castle, where a fundraising gala was taking place.'"

"Probably not. They likely would've said 'fatally shot.'"

"Assassinated sounds far more dignified, though, doesn't it?" I shook my entire body, much like a wet dog would. "Okay, change of subject. I can't talk about this anymore." I folded my arms. "What about you and Con?"

Her nostrils flared, and she made a growly noise in her throat. "The man makes me stark-raving mad."

"You seem to get on okay."

She shook her head. "Not at all. In fact, if I wouldn't be putting Ash out, I'd ask if I could stay here rather than at Blackmoor."

"I don't think he'd mind. There's another cottage. I quite liked it."

"You really think he'd be okay with it?"

"I don't see why not. And as far as your safety, it seems to me they've employed every available security officer in all of Scotland."

She rolled her eyes. "I noticed. There are more at Blackmoor. At Glenshadow too."

"So, every bodyguard in all of the UK."

"As it seems."

"David was surprised I noticed them."

Fallon laughed. "You're kidding."

I shook my head, hating that I'd been so standoffish with him. He'd saved my bloody life, and I'd shown my appreciation for it by giving him the cold shoulder. Well, I had *thanked* him. Many times, in fact. Still.

"I wonder if they're making progress."

Fallon looked at her watch. "It's been fifteen minutes. I'd say it's unlikely."

I stood and looked out the window. An older man was walking across the bridge, headed toward the castle. He turned when he reached the walkway that led to the entrance. "Who's that, I wonder?"

Fallon stood. "Perhaps Ash's uncle, Ambrose? I've heard stories about him from Con. None that were terribly interesting."

"He appears to be scowling."

"Hard to be the spare, I suppose. Then having it all passed down to one's nephew."

"You'd think he would've gotten over it by now."

"Does one ever?"

I returned to the table where my computer sat open. "I guess not. So, what should we be working on?"

Fallon glanced around the room as if she was looking to see if someone might overhear her. "I've been dying to tell you what I found in the monastery records."

"I'd forgotten all about those."

"Come over here, and I'll show you."

She pulled an image up on her laptop.

"What is that?" I asked.

"Drawings. Of tunnels."

My brow furrowed. "Tunnels?"

"They run beneath the three estates—Ashcroft, Glenshadow, and Blackmoor." More images appeared on the screen. "It's quite fascinating, is it not?"

"How old are these?" I asked, pointing at the screen.

"From what I read, they date back to the Jacobites."

I wished I was sitting in front of my computer, so I could quickly look it up. I was sure it was, or they were, something I'd learned about in history class.

"While most of the rebellion's battles took place closer to the Cairngorms in the eastern highlands, according to this, there was quite a stronghold here, in the west. It makes sense, given the proximity to the sea."

"I know it makes me sound like a bampot, but can you refresh my memory?"

Fallon smiled. "No worries. I had to look it all up too." She typed something into her computer, then turned the screen toward me. "Here, it's easier if you read it, which is all I'd be doing."

The article said that the Jacobite Rebellions were a series of uprisings that took place in Scotland between 1688 and 1746. While the time span was over several years, the rebellion's focus was first to restore James II, part of the Catholic Stuart dynasty, to the throne after William and Mary—Protestants—were crowned as co-monarchs of England, Scotland, and Ireland.

After James II's death, the rebellion continued in support of, first, his son, then his grandson.

"How does this relate to the tunnels?" I asked.

"Most believed they were urban legends, so to speak, but according to what I found, they were quite real. Perhaps they still are."

Fallon brought one of the maps back on the screen. "They were more commonly talked about in Edinburgh, where there are allegedly many vaults and passages, most of which predated the rebellions. There are several other castles that are purported to be connected to places that could serve as an escape route."

I raised my head. "Like Loch Fyne."

"Precisely."

"Err, do you think this relates to Weber and Tower-Meridian somehow?"

Fallon looked like a balloon I'd just stuck a pin in. "Sadly, no. Honestly, I just found it fascinating."

I jumped when I heard a rap at the door and looked up to see David on the threshold.

"What's wrong?" I asked, standing to approach him.

"Again, please forgive the interruption, but I must speak with you."

"Excuse me," I said to Fallon. "What's happened?" I asked once we were outside the library.

"Come with me. I can't speak about it here."

I followed him outside, to the waiting golf cart, then held on tight as he drove to Thistle Gate at a speed I didn't think the thing was capable of.

Once inside, he paced the small room. "I just had a conversation with my uncle, and he told me something that, I'll admit, I'm having a bit of a hard time processing."

"Come sit with me," I said, patting the sofa cushion.

"I'm not sure I can."

"Try."

He nodded, and when he sat down, I took his hands in mine.

"Okay, start at the beginning."

"It began innocently enough. Brose asked if he could see the cottage's refurbishments. On our way here, he mentioned my grandfather had always been enamored with the place." He looked down at our clasped hands. "That might've been the end of it, until he added, 'For good reason, I'd say.'"

"Go on."

"He assumed I knew, as he put it, about my grandfather and the housekeeper, whose name he couldn't remember."

"Agnes?" I gasped.

"Yes. Then he said, 'Angus and Agnes. The least well-kept secret in the west of Scotland.'"

My eyes opened wide. "Agnes is Mrs. Drummond's mother."

"And Gus—Angus—is her son."

I closed my eyes and pictured a family tree. "That would make Gus your what? Cousin?"

"And Mairi my aunt."

"Do you think they know?"

"Mairi, certainly. Gus, I rather hope he doesn't."

"Why not?" I asked.

"One, that he kept it from me. Or worse, that he believed I knew and never acknowledged our, err, familial relationship."

"He'd never think that of you."

"No?"

I shook my head. "No. Absolutely not."

"I hope you're right."

"What will you do now?"

"I suppose I need to confront Mairi. Good God, on Christmas of all days." He pulled his hands away and reached into his pocket. "This, you really won't believe." He opened the watch I'd given him. "Ambrose took this from my grandfather. In essence, he stole it."

"No!"

David nodded. "He turned the same ashen shade Mrs. Drummond, err, Mairi did when she first saw it."

"My God," I said under my breath.

"There's more, not that it's as significant."

"Tell me anyway." He took my hands in his again. "I asked Ambrose if he'd ever been in love, and he told me once. To my mother."

This time, I withdrew a hand and covered my mouth.

"He brought her here, and she and my father promptly fell in love, to Brose's great heartbreak."

"How awful. Sorry, I know she was your mum, but…"

"He said neither of them knew his feelings, but no wonder he and my dad never got on."

"Admittedly, my head is spinning. I can't imagine how you must feel."

"Hence the pacing."

I smiled. "You must speak with Gus."

He nodded. "I don't know where to begin."

"The same way you told me," I suggested.

"But what if he has no idea—like me?"

"Good point. It would be best to speak with Mairi first."

"My aunt, who is now overseeing the preparation of our Christmas dinner. The one she's never been invited to share with her own family. God, he was a bastard. Err, I don't mean it that way. I mean, my grandfather was, you know."

"I know who you meant and how you meant it."

His expression softened. "Of course you did. I was frantic to speak with you, knowing you'd understand."

I leaned forward and kissed him. "So. Mairi. You must speak with her *before* dinner."

"Agreed."

"Let's go."

His head cocked. "Where?"

"Back to the castle. You'll hardly be able to get her to come down here again."

"Right." He stood and pulled me up with him.

"Oh, one more thing before I forget. Fallon expressed an interest in staying here rather than at Blackmoor."

He stared at me in a way that seemed like he had no idea what I was talking about.

"She said Con drives her 'stark-raving mad.'"

"He would do. As with most people."

"I assured her you wouldn't mind. I hope I didn't overstep."

"Of course you didn't. So, um, here?" He motioned with his hand. "At Thistle Gate?"

"Actually, I suggested Primrose Croft."

He let out the breath he'd been holding. "Yes. Absolutely. She's more than welcome. Although I have a feeling Con will not be happy about it."

"That's his problem."

David smiled. "Precisely."

23

Savior

There were several ways I thought to broach the subject of who Mairi and Gus were to me once we reached the castle, but as soon as we walked in the door, my mind went blank.

"David?" Sullivan whispered when I stood, frozen, in the entryway.

"I…I can't…" I stammered.

"We can. Come, we'll do it together."

God, I loved her for saying we instead of me alone. While I'd been able to rely on Con, Tag, and especially my cousin, Gus, the support I felt from Sullivan was different. It was almost like she was an extension of me. One I had no idea how I'd lived this long without.

"Yes. We can do this," I repeated.

"Ask her to meet us in the library. Tell her there's something I want to ask her about."

"Yes. Good. I like that idea."

"I'll go make sure Fallon isn't still in there."

"Again, good. Thanks."

Before she walked away, Sullivan squeezed my hand, leaned up, and kissed me. "I love you," she whispered.

I squared my shoulders and marched into the largest of the two kitchens, where I knew Christmas dinner was being prepared. Then, in my most duke-like tone of voice, said, "Mrs. Drummond? A word?"

She looked about the room at those fast at work, then wiped her hands on the apron she wore. "Of course, my lord."

"In the library, if you will. Sullivan has something, err, to ask about."

"Sir, can it wait—"

"It cannot."

Her eyes widened at my tone, but I had no choice. If she didn't walk out of the kitchen with me right now, I might lose my nerve, and that wasn't something I could do. There was no way I'd be able to sit at the table, enjoying Christmas dinner, and hide my unease. Especially from Gus. He'd pick up on it and perhaps make the wrong assumptions. Like I had with Brose all these years.

I led the way, and thankfully, she followed. Once inside, I closed the two large doors that likely hadn't been shut in years, based on how they creaked. Sullivan was seated by the fireplace, where I noticed there were three chairs rather than two. All had been scooted so they were within inches of the others.

"Please take a seat," I said to Mairi, motioning to the middle chair.

"Sir? What is this about?" She'd gone ghostly white.

"There's something I need to ask you about."

Mairi nodded. "Yes, sir."

"First, I insist you call me Ash. Or David. Whichever you prefer."

While she nodded a second time, she didn't speak.

"Mairi…What I mean to say is Aunt Mairi. Does Gus know?"

Her eyes flooded with tears, and she gasped to catch her breath before a sob came from somewhere deep inside her. I reached out and took her hand at the same time Sullivan did her other.

Mairi hung her head, trying several times to catch her breath. Finally, she looked up at me. "You were never meant to know. This morning… It's my fault, isn't it? That you figured it out?"

I took a deep breath and shook my head. "As my dear cousin pointed out to me—or maybe it was Con, probably both—I lack the simplest of investigative skills." I looked over at Sullivan. My eyes pleading for her to speak.

"It was Ambrose."

Mairi turned her head to face Sullivan. "I begged him not to." She choked on another sob. "Why now? Today?"

"He and I were at Thistle Gate, and he reminisced about how much my grandfather loved the place. I don't think he necessarily meant to divulge the secret it seems everyone knew but me. Well, Con and Tag didn't know, either—"

"What David means to say is Ambrose shared the familial connection between you, your son, and himself."

"Aye," Mairi said, turning to face me again. "I am so sorry, sir—"

"No. I am not sir to you. Never again," I snapped, then immediately felt awful. "Apologies. I just cannot bear the idea that my aunt, the only one I've ever had, has been put in the position of referring to me as such. It breaks my heart."

Both Sullivan and Mairi teared up.

"Apologies," I repeated. "And as much as I wish we could toss the whole bloody Christmas meal out the window." Mairi's face scrunched. "Sorry, I didn't mean that. Rather, that's to say, I wish you didn't need to return to the kitchens, but I certainly understand why you do. You and I together will determine how the staff is informed." Something occurred to me. "Unless they all know." The idea pained me.

"*Nae.* No one knows." She hung her head again. "Not even my beloved Angus."

"Forgive me for saying this, but are you certain? Unlike me, he is quite natural in deducing most anything."

"He is smart, like his grandfather."

"And you," I added. "Did you know him well?"

"I did not. There were times my mum and I would visit Thistle Gate. Certainly not often. The last was the day before he died. He wasn't ill, but I think my mum sensed it."

"I'm glad you got to say goodbye, even if it wasn't with those words."

She nodded, then smiled. "I spent most of my life terrified of the man."

I smiled too. "I understand. Completely."

"Gus," Sullivan whispered.

"Right."

"Can we wait to tell him? Tomorrow, perhaps?" Mairi asked.

I shook my head. "I cannot wait. I cannot be with him knowing who he is to me and not divulge it."

"He'll never forgive me."

"You're wrong," said Sullivan. "He'll understand. I know he will."

Mairi's expression was hopeful. "It would be my Christmas wish that he would."

I glanced up and saw him through the window. Neither woman was facing that direction. "Excuse me. I'll be right back."

I raced out of the library, then toward the foyer. I arrived at the same time Gus removed his coat. When our eyes met, he nodded barely perceptibly. "You know."

"Just today. A short while ago," I assured him.

"I believe you."

"I've just spoken with your mum."

"How is she?"

"Quite worried about your reaction." I took a step closer. "Gus, if you knew, why didn't you tell me?"

"It wasn't until I saw the photo of the two of us in his study that I believed it might be true. Even then,

I wasn't certain. Then this morning, the way my mum reacted."

"Yes. Sullivan picked up on it."

He smiled. "You did as well."

I chuckled. "And yet when Ambrose told me, I was stunned."

"Ambrose, eh?"

I recounted what I'd told Mairi about my uncle wanting to see what we'd done to the cottage. "I don't think he intended to tell me."

"He's not had an easy go of it. That's not to say he doesn't drive me mad."

"A sentiment shared by most." I sighed. "Your mum is probably in agony presently."

"Where is she?"

"The library. With Sullivan. Oh, and I told her it would be her decision as to how the staff is informed. Although the idea of her serving us dinner doesn't sit right with me."

Gus nodded. "I dare say it will be easier for her that way. Falling into the role she's played most of her life."

"Understood. Come." I motioned for him to follow me. "You go in first," I said once we reached the library.

The moment she saw him, Mairi jumped from her chair and rushed over to him. When he held out his arms, she fell into his embrace.

"Forgive me," she said through her tears.

"Nothing to forgive, Mum."

"I should've told you. I kept the secret all these years."

"You did what you had to do, and no one, including Ash, faults you for it."

"He's right," I added when she raised her gaze to mine. "There is the matter of dinner."

She gasped. "Yes. I must return to the kitchens."

"That isn't what I meant. I will leave the decision to you. However, there will be a place for you at the table this evening. If you're not ready for everyone to know, I will respect that. Just know that I very much want you to join us."

"Thank you, sir, err, David."

I loved that only she and Sullivan used my given name. It felt right.

"Shall we set an extra place at the table?" Gus asked.

"Thank you, but not this year, son."

He nodded. "Understood." He held out his arm, and she took it. "Be right back," he said over his shoulder.

As soon as they were out of the room, Sullivan stood, then we walked toward each other and embraced. "I think that went well, didn't you?" she asked.

"As well as could be expected."

"Gus knew?"

"He suspected, but this morning confirmed it for him."

"Is he angry with her?"

"Not at all. He understands the position she's been in all these years."

Sullivan hugged me tighter. "I love that the two of you have been so close."

"I do as well. He's the brother I never had. I feel that in my heart."

"As do I," I heard Gus say from the doorway.

I released Sullivan, and he and I embraced. "Can we sit for a moment?" I asked.

He shut the library doors and joined Sullivan and me in front of the fireplace, where she sat between us.

"I'd rather no one know until my mum decides she's ready," he began.

"I'll respect that decision."

"Which means you cannot let on." His eyes bored into mine, and I laughed.

"I am quickly learning my faults this Christmas."

"Not a fault. A weakness." He winked.

"I suppose you've been compensating for them my entire life."

Gus' expression softened. "As you have for me."

"We're a good team, cousin."

He nodded. "We are, Ash. We've always been."

While we agreed not to say anything to Con or Tag, the one thing I had to do at dinner was raise my glass in a toast. "To family," I said, my eyes meeting Gus'.

At the meal's conclusion, I invited everyone to join me in the library, where I'd requested dessert be served as a buffet so everyone could pick and choose as they liked. When I saw Fallon standing off on her own, I approached.

"I understand you'd like to relocate."

Her eyes met mine. "If it wouldn't be an inconvenience."

"None at all." I followed her line of sight to where Con stood. "Is he aware?"

"I broached the subject, saying I thought it might be easier for Sullivan and me to work together."

"Was he amenable?"

"He seems to be."

Con looked over at us, and I raised my glass of brandy. While he did the same, something told me he would rather have flipped me off. "Disappointed, perhaps?" I asked.

"I don't know why he would be. All we do is argue."

I raised a brow.

"Mostly."

"The choice is yours. Should you prefer to stay here, you're more than welcome."

"I appreciate it."

Before I could join Sullivan, Tag, Con, and Gus intercepted me. "A word?" Tag asked.

"Here or elsewhere?"

"Here. However, discreetly," he responded.

"Go ahead."

"I've spoken with my contact in Syria," he said in a hushed tone.

We moved to the opposite side of the room from where the two women stood. "What did you learn?" I asked.

"Several things. First, Eric Weber doesn't exist, according to the Syrian government."

"Difficult to offer diplomatic protection to a ghost. He operates under an alias, I presume?"

"Not that I've yet been able to uncover one. What is confusing is that the immunity is in the name we know him as."

"True. What else?"

"According to my source, the man without a name has close ties to Syrian military intelligence."

"Nightingale also has reason to believe he's met with both Russian and Chinese military leaders."

Tag glared at Con. Perhaps he hadn't wanted his source named. Although I couldn't see a reason why he wouldn't want me to know. I glanced over at Fallon and Sullivan, who were in the midst of their own conversation and likely hadn't overheard.

"Does your source know what about?"

Tag shook his head. "Only that the most logical theory would be biological or chemical weapons development." He turned to Con.

"I had minimal luck with the encrypted emails we believe were to or from Weber. While I can't prove either, some of what I read confirmed an unknown suspect's ties to Russia and China. Not those two countries alone, however."

"Who else?"

"Those you would predict. Allies of either or both."

"Any signs that they're working together against a common enemy?" I asked.

Gus raised a brow. "Aren't they always?"

"I suppose that's a given. What else?"

"There's mention of a secret research facility."

My eyes widened. "Where?"

Con raised a brow.

"Apologies. It would obviously not be secret if you knew."

"There was one other I found of particular interest. While the evidence is very vague, I suspect he may be playing both sides against each other. Meaning, the UK's allies versus the combined efforts of Russia and China."

"He would do, wouldn't he?" I muttered.

"The most important piece of information in that communication is a name—Labyrinth."

"He toys with the demise of civilization," I said under my breath.

"You may be right," Con said with a heavy sigh.

"How much of this does Fallon know?" I asked.

"None."

"Is there a reason she and Sullivan shouldn't be made aware?"

"Tag, Gus, and I discussed it. The decision to either share or withhold information must be unanimous."

"Appreciated. I'm in favor of looping them in."

"As am I," said Gus.

"Shall I assume the two of you are opposed?"

"Not necessarily," said Con.

"But?"

When neither Con nor Tag spoke, Gus did. "They're worried about a leak."

I shook my head. "The NDA."

"Versus the biggest and perhaps most important story of their careers?" said Con.

"I don't believe it's about their careers." I glanced at the women a second time. "What do you suggest?"

"We brief them on the Russian and Chinese connection as well as Weber's yet undiscovered secret identity."

"And leave out the project name?"

Con nodded. "As well as the UK connection."

I cocked my head. "That part does seem somewhat obvious. The UK is Tower-Meridian's base of operation."

"Which is why it makes the most sense that the secret research facility is here."

"Meaning in Scotland?"

"Yes," he responded.

"It gives us something to go on, which makes me think six heads are better than four. Meaning—"

"We know what you mean, Ash," snapped Tag.

"Apologies," I said, noticing both women raised their heads. I leaned in closer. "The danger is they're both intuitive enough to know we're holding something back. In which case, they may do the same."

"While none of us has influence over Fallon, you do with Sullivan, Ash," said Gus.

"I'll speak with her. But first, do we all agree that, if I deem it appropriate, I will divulge what you've told me?"

"Agreed," said Gus.

"Agreed," said Con, although in a more reluctant tone.

All eyes turned to Tag.

He lowered his head and shook it. "I'm against it. However, in order to move forward, we must be unanimous."

"Are we, then?" I asked.

"We are," he responded.

24

Sullivan

"Don't look, but they know something," said Fallon. "And they're not including us in the conversation."

It pained me to agree, but she was right. I willed David to call us over, to include us, but they continued speaking in hushed tones without doing so.

"Bloody hell," Fallon muttered. "I *knew* he'd do this."

"Con?"

"Of course—the bastard. He's been behaving strangely since we returned to Blackmoor earlier. I cannot abide that man."

"As David said, you're welcome to stay here instead."

"And I will do. But first, I need to give *Conrad* a piece of my mind."

"What do you say we call it a night?" Con asked when all three men approached us.

Fallon glared at him. "Fine," she practically spat.

"Reconvene in the morning?" Tag asked.

Fallon folded her arms. "I'll need to be here at eight."

"As in zero eight hundred?" Con asked.

Fallon rolled her eyes. "Yes, and if it's a problem, I can make other arrangements."

"It's not a problem as much as it is bloody early," he said under his breath.

After saying good night, Ash and I took the golf cart back to Thistle Gate.

"Did you happen to notice the design on the entrance to the cottage?" he asked.

"On the gate?"

"Yes."

"I did. It's quite beautiful. Do you know who did it?"

"I do not. And can you believe that, until earlier today, I didn't notice the thistles?"

I had to cover my mouth to stifle my laugh. "Is that not where it got its name?"

David shrugged and sighed. "No idea."

"What's this about?" I asked after we'd parked and were nearing the front door.

"Apparently, I score very low on both observation and investigative skills."

"I disagree."

"I appreciate it, but don't feel as though you have to placate me."

I opened the door, and we went inside.

"You recognized me and saved my life. Anyone who says you aren't observant is out of their mind."

I took off my coat and slung it on the back of the sofa. When David's fists were clenched at his sides and it looked like he might have even been biting the inside of his cheek, I picked it up and hung it on the coat rack instead. "Sorry."

"There's nothing to apologize for."

"Now, that I hung it up."

"Sorry?"

"My coat."

David held out his hand and led me to the sofa. "There are things we need to discuss."

"Tonight?"

"As much as I'd like to put it off, I don't think it would be wise to do so."

"Is this what you were discussing in the library after dinner?"

"Yes."

"Then, you're right. You should tell me."

"As you know, Tag has a contact in Syria. What he was able to learn was that, according to their government, there is no such person as Eric Weber."

"He obviously uses an alias. Perhaps more than one."

"Agreed. Except the diplomatic protection he has via Syria is in the name of Eric Weber."

My brow furrowed. "That is curious."

"Secondly, he has ties to Syrian military intelligence, and she believes he has met with both the Russian and Chinese governments."

"She?"

"Err, yes. His source."

"Go on."

"The logical theory as far as what he's shipping is either biological or chemical weapons."

I disagreed, but I'd wait until he was finished to comment.

"From what Con was able to decipher from encrypted emails, Weber may also be working with the UK and our allies. And finally, he believes there's evidence of a secret research facility."

"Here in Scotland."

"There's no evidence pointing to it specifically."

"Except the shipments all originate here. It's the only logical explanation."

"Perhaps. There's one more bit. The name Labyrinth, which Con believes is the project."

"A complicated and irregular network of passages."

"Yes, that is the definition."

My mind raced with what Fallon had told me about the tunnels earlier. Not so much the ones here, but throughout Scotland—in Edinburgh, in particular.

"Sullivan?"

I realized I'd gotten lost in thought. "Sorry, did you say something?"

"No, but I expected you would."

"Right. Apologies. Again. Thank you for telling me all of this."

His eyes scrunched. "And yet, there's something you're not telling me."

"Not specifically."

David stood and paced. "You must understand that this is not something you can report on."

Ah. That was at the crux of the odd behavior. "Without my investigation, you'd know nothing about Weber or Tower-Meridian."

"That isn't entirely true."

"Let me rephrase. If you hadn't been sent to *kill* me that night, Weber wouldn't be on your radar or SIS'."

He put his hands on his hips. "Perhaps not mine."

"So what you're saying is everything you told me tonight is off the record and I'm not permitted to make use of it."

"I'll remind you of the NDA you signed."

I stood as well, unsure what to do or where to go, only that I couldn't continue this conversation. I stalked from the room and went past the bedroom we'd shared in search of another.

"What are you doing?" he asked when I returned to the other bedroom and pulled several things from the drawers.

"Relocating."

"Sullivan, don't be absurd—"

I stomped my feet on the way back to the other bedroom, which seemed to shut him up. Before I could shut the door, he put his arm out and kept it open.

"We're in the midst of a conversation. I insist we finish it."

"You just informed me I could not report on my own bloody story, *Ashcroft*. My story. How dare you? And then, you had the audacity to remind me that I'd signed an NDA. As if I would've forgotten. Again, *how dare you*?"

"Is that your intention, then? To report on this?"

"Yes."

He wove his fingers in his hair. "I cannot believe this."

"There's another question you should've asked, David. In fact, there is none more important."

"What?"

I walked over to the door. "Please leave."

"What is the other question?"

"I'd like to be alone."

"Sullivan, please, just tell me."

I shook my head. "When you've figured it out, let me know."

"And in the meantime, I cannot be with you?"

The way he'd phrased the question, the tone of his voice, had me so close to giving in. But I couldn't. For a relationship to work between us, David needed to respect me, and that meant respect my work. I loved him, but I couldn't be with someone who treated me— as an investigative journalist—with such little regard.

"Wait," he said when I put my hand on his chest to push him out of the way. "I may not know the question, but I do know this."

I sighed. "Go on."

"If you report on what we've learned now, two things will happen. One, Weber will know we're on to him and perhaps very close to exposing his crimes. That is the least important of the two. What matters more is that you will face even greater danger, and if anything happens to you, if I'm unable to keep you safe, if…" His voice caught. "Sullivan, without you, my life wouldn't be worth living." He whispered the last of his words.

I put my other hand on his chest but didn't push with either. "David, the question you didn't ask but should've is *when*."

"When?"

"Yes. *When* do I intend to file the story."

"What is the answer, Sullivan?"

"When the story is finished. When Weber is either behind bars or dead. When we know what Labyrinth is and that it has been dismantled—or whatever needs to happen with or to it." I paused. "David, the bottom line is, releasing this story now wouldn't just put my own life at greater risk. It would affect all of us here, working on it. Do you really think I'd put a story before so many lives?"

"Put that way, no, I don't believe you would." He sighed. "Earlier, when we were in the library, I commented that Weber is toying with the demise of civilization."

"I agree."

He studied me. "You don't think it's chemical or biological weaponry, do you?"

"I do not. However, what I fear it is, is almost too terrifying to even consider."

"Will you tell me?"

"If we're going to continue this discussion, we need to sit down. But first, a drink."

David grabbed the decanter and two glasses and sat beside me on the sofa in the living room. "I'll get the fire going again."

"Thank you," I said, pouring half glasses for each of us.

He sat down and raised his. "To us."

"To us," I repeated but with scrunched eyes.

"The two people who intend to prevent Weber from destroying civilization as we know it."

I smiled. "Yes. To us."

"So, what *do* you think Weber is trafficking?"

"The only thing that makes sense is AIWS— Autonomous Intelligent Weapons Systems."

David set his glass on the table and put his head in his hands. "Good God."

"Yes," I whispered. "Good God."

25

Savior

"Argh," I groaned, wishing we hadn't agreed to a zero-eight-hundred start time today. I doubted I'd slept more than one hour. Sullivan probably hadn't gotten much more rest than that.

"Go back to sleep," she mumbled.

"We cannot. Fallon is arriving at eight, remember?"

"Bloody hell," she moaned, rolling over. We hadn't made love last night or this morning, and while I'd say *yet*, we had very little time to dress and report to the castle as it was. My body—my cock, in particular—ached with need.

"David?"

"Yes, my love?"

"Can you please contact Con and ask him to delay?"

As much as I wanted to give in and do as she asked, there was an urgency, based on Sullivan's theory about AIWS, that couldn't be ignored.

"You know we cannot."

She rolled to face me. "You're a taskmaster."

"And you're a brilliant, beautiful, inquisitive, investigative genius."

"Compliments will not get me out of bed any faster. In fact, the opposite is true."

When I stood and held out my hand, her eyes traveled the length of my body, stopping at my midsection.

"We could take a quick shower," she suggested.

"I fear the only way that would help is if it's ice cold." I wiggled my fingers. "Come. The sooner the meeting is over, the sooner we can return to our love nest."

"How can I deny such sweetness?" She scooted closer to where I stood.

When she got up and pressed her nakedness next to mine, I suddenly didn't care if we kept the others waiting all damned day. "A shower it is," I said, pulling her with me.

"Only if it's warm."

"Not warm, Sullivan. It will be scorchingly hot."

She rolled her eyes but followed me anyway.

"Ready?" I asked when we were about to leave for the castle.

"Not really. The truth is, beyond my theory, I don't know that much about AI and how it relates to weaponry. What if they all think I'm crazy?"

"I don't think you're crazy. That must count for something."

"Of course it does."

"Like everything else, we'll present it to the group for consideration and see where it leads. Okay?"

"Okay. Oh, and there's one other thing."

"Yes?"

"Labyrinths."

"Go on."

"While at Glenshadow, Fallon found monastery records that showed drawings of an elaborate system of tunnels believed to have been built during the Jacobite Rebellion. That led us to consider what others exist in Scotland, primarily in Edinburgh. According to her research, there are endless passageways that some believe are urban myths, but others believe are functional to the point they're still being used."

"You said Fallon found drawings of tunnels while at Glenshadow?"

"That's right. Why?"

"A few days ago, before we left for Glenshadow, Con, Gus, Tag, and I were reviewing the plans for the cottage. This cottage. One page of the drawings was of a similar tunnel system."

"David, I don't think—"

"Hear me out."

"Sorry. Go on."

"During the discussion, Con hinted that Gus already knew about tunnels that led from the castle to this cottage. Gus denied it, of course."

"You think it's Mairi who knows."

"I do. She might even know something about those in Edinburgh. If she doesn't, I'd be willing to bet she knows someone else who does."

"Brilliant, David. See? You're not so bad at investigative work, after all."

I checked the time and groaned. "We best be on our way. It's half eight already."

"There you two are. We thought you'd forgotten our meeting," said Con when we joined them in the castle's library.

"Yes, well, we're here now, aren't we?" I snapped. "If you recall, I was not the one to suggest we meet at this ungodly hour." I looked about the room. "By the way, where is Fallon?"

"Here," she said, walking with a tray of fruit. Mairi followed with pastries.

"Bless you," I said, wishing I could reveal who she really was to me. However, I wouldn't push. Telling the Ashcroft staff would not be easy for her.

I poured tea for both Sullivan and me, then sat beside her. "Are you ready to get started?"

"I am, but I'm wondering if we should ask Mrs. Drummond, err, Mairi to sit in or if we should wait until we're ready to discuss the Edinburgh tunnels."

Given even the most seasoned intelligence agents in the room would likely be shocked by Sullivan's theories, I couldn't imagine how Mairi might react. "I think it would be best to wait."

"Right."

"If I could have everyone's attention, we have a great deal to discuss this morning. Before we do, has everyone been briefed on the information Tag relayed last evening?"

Fallon was among those murmuring they had, which was all I'd wanted to be certain of.

"One of the things discussed was, if our theory is correct that Weber is trafficking weaponry, it would stand to reason it would either be chemical or biological. Sullivan brought up another option worth consideration."

She cleared her throat. "We're all in agreement that Weber knows a well-timed and targeted raid on even one of Tower-Meridian's shipments would put an end to his operation. I'd like to suggest we consider that it might not."

"What do you mean?" Fallon asked.

"If what he's developing is something we've never seen or know nothing about, then a raid would be fruitless."

I knew the moment Con realized what she was about to suggest. He sat back in his chair, raised his hands to his head, and briefly closed his eyes. "Bloody fucking hell," he said under his breath.

"What am I missing?" Fallon asked.

"Keep in mind what I'd about to suggest is considered science fiction presently and I doubt very much it's reached the stage of more advanced development."

Sullivan took a deep breath and let it out slowly. "What if Tower-Meridian is trafficking AI weaponry or rather, AI weapons systems?"

My eyes met Con's, and he nodded.

"Good Lord," Fallon said, leaning against her chair like Con had. "Do you truly think it's possible?"

"It is," Con responded. "Terrifyingly so."

"You mentioned Labyrinth as a possible project code name," said Sullivan.

Fallon raised her head. "Are you suggesting Weber is using tunnel systems for transport?"

"A logical assumption," Con commented.

"What exactly are AI weapons systems?" Fallon asked.

Sullivan looked at Con. "You'd be better able to explain than I would."

He nodded. "Think about the technology in the same way you would drones. The difference being that there isn't a need for a person to be sitting in a bunker, making decisions about what the drone should do. Instead, neural weapon controls—self-learning combat systems, if you will—would be employed."

"With no oversight?" Fallon asked.

"Not necessarily. However, AI systems could adapt and employ battlefield strategies instantaneously, among many, many other things."

His somber tone was indicative of the mood in the room.

Fallon's eyes widened. "Are you suggesting military organizations are already employing these technologies?"

"No, not extensively anyway. To put it in perspective, it took what was then the USSR four years to establish nuclear weapons after the US first developed the capabilities."

"But you believe Weber is already selling it to Russia and China," Fallon pressed.

"Possessing the technology to put a man on the moon is quite different than successfully launching a rocket," Con countered.

"But it's only a matter of time."

It was like watching a tennis ball being volleyed between the two. However, if Fallon hadn't been the one to ask the questions, someone else would have.

"Yes, it's only a matter of time. Which means, Weber must be stopped." Con looked up at me. "This is bigger than us, Ash."

I agreed. "I'll alert Typhon."

"Viper as well, and they'll need to come to us," said Gus.

"Roger that," I responded.

Fallon stood. "I need to do something productive, or I'll go mad."

"I'd like to explore the tunnel idea more in depth," Sullivan offered.

Fallon nodded.

I turned to Gus. "Regarding tunnel systems, Con alluded to you being an expert on them."

Gus raised a brow and smirked. "He did no such thing, and you know it."

"Who, then?"

"Sod off, Ash." He got up and left the room, but I expected he'd be back within a few minutes.

"Gentlemen, should we leave the library to the ladies?" I asked while we waited for Gus to return.

"Good idea," said Tag.

"Be there in a minute," said Con, approaching Fallon after I kissed Sullivan's cheek and Tag followed me out of the room.

"What's going on with those two?" I asked.

Tag chuckled. "While our friend knows more about AI weapons systems, Fallon knows more about everything else."

"Kicking his ego to the curb, is she?"

"No more than Sullivan is yours."

"Excellent point. However, I'm in love, mate."

"You don't say?"

"Don't say what?" Con asked.

I smirked. "That Fallon is more intelligent than you are."

"In what universe?"

"What are you gents talking about?" asked Gus, who'd come in and shut the door behind him.

"Fallon is smarter than Con," Tag responded.

"No question."

"While you're all terribly amusing, need I remind you of the matter at hand?"

"You're right, Con. Let's get down to business," I said, taking a seat and motioning for them to as well.

26

Sullivan

Mairi looked between Fallon and me when Gus brought her into the library.

"Thank you for joining us, Mrs. Drummond," I said, hoping that, by addressing her more formally, she'd know Fallon wasn't aware of the family connection between her and David.

"I'm Mairi to you," she said, winking.

"I appreciate it, Mairi," I said, winking back.

"If you don't need me, I'll head off to where the boys are meeting," said Gus as he walked toward the door.

"Close it behind you, if you would, please," said Fallon, turning from him to his mum. "So, Mairi, is it?"

"Aye," she responded, folding her arms and pursing her lips.

This conversation was not off to a good start. "Fallon, why don't you begin by explaining what you stumbled on while you were at Glenshadow," I suggested, hoping that by inserting myself between the two women, tensions would ease.

"Right. So, I've always been fascinated with old books and libraries, of course. This one in particular is quite lovely." Something felt off with Fallon's approach. It was almost as if she was trying too hard to win the woman over. Or perhaps what I was picking up on felt too much like condescension. Either way, I didn't like it.

"If I may interrupt?"

Mairi turned to face me. "Of course, luv."

"What Fallon found were maps in what appeared to be a record book dating back to when Glenshadow was still a monastery. I believe we have scans of some of them."

"Aye?" Mairi sat up straighter and rested her arms on the table. "I'd like to see them."

Fallon turned her computer around.

"According to this and others she found in the same book, there used to be a tunnel system that connected Ashcroft, Glenshadow, and Blackmoor."

"I wouldn't know anything about that."

"What about in Edinburgh?" Fallon asked.

"Nae. Nothing about those either."

"Would you happen to know anyone who does?" I asked.

Mairi looked up at the ceiling for a few seconds, then back at me. "No one comes to mind, lass."

"Okay. Well, thank you, anyway."

"Hang on. What about those here, at Ashcroft? Surely, you know about those," Fallon pressed.

I clenched my fists when Mairi bristled and turned to me. "Sorry, I'm not much help, luv."

Fallon pushed away from the table and stood by the window.

"We certainly appreciate your help, though."

She reached over and patted my hand. "Of course, my lady." When my eyes scrunched, she shook her head and winked after glancing over to make sure Fallon was still facing the other direction.

I stood and walked her out. "We'll speak later," she whispered. When she closed the door behind her and I turned around, Fallon was facing me.

"What was that all about?"

My head cocked. "What do you mean?"

"What did she say to you just then?"

"That we'd speak later. I'm sure she was just being polite."

"She's lying."

I had to admit I thought the same thing. However, what I couldn't understand was why.

"What do you know about Ambrose Ashcroft?" Fallon asked.

The abrupt change of subject jarred me. "Err, not much at all. Why?"

"My understanding from Con is that he and Mairi are quite close."

I thought it over for a minute. "I suppose that would explain why he's here so often. I've not met him."

"I did earlier. There's something about the two of them that doesn't sit right with me."

"What are you suggesting?" I asked.

"Clearly, she's hiding something. I picked up on it yesterday."

Fallon was right, but it wasn't at all what she was thinking. However, without Mairi's permission to do so, I wouldn't feel right about divulging her secret.

"I can't believe this," I heard her mumble.

I looked up and realized she was studying me.

"Now, you're holding something back. This won't do, Sullivan. Either we work together, or we don't. I told you I was willing to consider you for the exec-editor-of-investigations job, but if you aren't willing to share what you know, I truly don't see how I'll be able to move you into that position."

I bristled and wanted to remind her that she was the one who'd brought up the promotion. I certainly hadn't asked for it. "What I know has nothing to do with the tunnels or with the Weber investigation. It's a personal matter I'm not at liberty to share."

Fallon sighed, pulled out her chair, and sat down. She was silent for several minutes, then leaned forward and rested her arms on the table. "Forgive me. Tensions are running high for all of us. It wasn't my intention to take it out on you."

"Thank you."

"I cannot spend one more night at Blackmoor. That man—*argh*—my nerves are simply frayed." She reached across the table for my hand, but I didn't extend it. "Forgive me?"

"Of course."

"Back to the drawing board, as they say."

She stood and walked toward one of the book-shelves that lined the walls. "So, if there were tunnels, you'd think a room such as this would be the ideal way to access them. Behind a bookcase, perhaps?"

We both laughed since, with the exception of the fireplace and the windows, all four walls were covered with them.

"I need a bathroom break. Shall I check in with the boys, or do you want to?"

"Go ahead. I'd like to see what else there might be online about the Jacobites in Edinburgh."

"Sounds good."

Before I reopened my laptop, I stood to stretch. There was a wee view of Thistle Gate from out the window, but to see much more, I'd have to stand on a chair.

I thought about my first couple of days here and how I'd noticed CCTV cameras camouflaged within the low stone walls lining both sides of the pathways. Maybe the tunnels followed the same directions.

I also couldn't help but wonder what in the world was up with Mairi. Like Fallon, I'd sensed she was lying, but why would she? Granted, even I didn't care for Fallon's approach. It didn't seem like enough of a reason for her not to be honest, though.

Just as I took a seat and opened my computer, an instant message popped up on the screen. It was from Clive.

You're in grave danger. Make contact immediately before it's too late.

"Bloody hell," I muttered, turning when I heard a noise behind me. "Fallon, you are not going to believe this—"

I glanced over my shoulder, but instead of the woman I expected to see, a man dressed all in black and wearing a mask put his hand over my mouth and nose. He lifted me from the chair with his arm around my waist, and carried me through a passageway behind a bookshelf that was no longer flush against the wall. He eased past the panel that closed behind us, and we descended into darkness. My screams were muffled by his glove, and while I kicked with all my might to get free, with him cutting off my source of oxygen, my energy was waning quickly.

27

Savior

"How goes it with the tunnels?" I asked Mairi when she rapped on the office door, then came in.

"May I have a word, sir?"

My eyes scrunched, and I glanced over at Gus.

"Mum, what's wrong?"

"I need to speak with the two of you urgently," she whispered, leading us out into the hallway.

"What is it?" I asked.

"It's Miss Fallon…I don't have a good feeling."

"Can you be more specific?" Gus asked.

"Earlier, I thought I saw her speaking with Ambrose, and then she was asking about the tunnels. It just didn't feel right."

"Odd that she was speaking with Brose, but it was Sullivan who requested they meet with you about the tunnels. Are they still in the library?" I asked.

"Yes, sir, err, David."

"Let's pay them a visit, shall we?"

As we got closer, I noticed the library door was open. When I rushed inside and found it empty, a cold terror coursed through my body.

"Where are they?" Gus asked.

"Look!" Mairi pointed to where the books in one of the cases were askew. A couple had fallen to the floor. "It could be a passageway to the tunnels."

"How in the bloody hell does this open?" I shouted, rushing over to it.

Mairi came up behind me and began tossing books to the floor. "There should be a latch behind here, somewhere."

"This?" Gus asked, putting his hand on a metal lever.

"Yes! Stand back," Mairi shouted.

"What's going on?" Con asked, racing into the room with Tag just as the case swung open.

"Sullivan's gone. We think she's been taken into the tunnels."

"Come with me," he said to Tag. "We can head them off from Thistle Gate." The two raced out of the room.

"This way," said Mairi, motioning for us to follow her through the dark opening.

I pulled my mobile out, turned on the spotlight, and readied my weapon. Gus did the same.

We were a few paces inside when we came to a fork. "You go that way. I'll go the other," I said to Gus, pointing to the right.

"Nae, go left," said Mairi from behind me.

"Are you certain?"

"Aye. We only go to the left." She said it almost by rote, as though she was repeating something she'd been told again and again.

Narrow steps led to long corridors, which led to more narrow stairways. "You're sure this is the right way?" I asked, not hearing any sound in the dark, damp corridors that grew narrower as we went.

"Yes, this way." She'd lowered her voice to a whisper. "Shh. Listen."

It was faint, but I could hear people shouting.

"It's not much farther."

I'd just rounded a bend in the passageway when I heard a woman's blood-curdling scream. I couldn't say why, but something in my gut told me it wasn't Sullivan. I raced forward, cocked my gun, aimed, and fired.

28

Sullivan

I came to, gasping and trying to catch my breath when the man dropped me on the stone floor.

"I hate that it's come to this." I heard a woman's voice say at the same time I felt the sharp jab of the toe of her shoe in my side. "Had you simply played along, things would've gone so much better for you. As it is, you've signed your own death warrant, along with the rest of them."

Still gasping, I got to my hands and knees and slowly raised my head, fighting against the darkness that threatened to take me back under.

"My God, you've been working for Weber all along?"

"That no longer matters. You're finished. Sullivan."

As Fallon raised the gun, I lunged with all the energy I could muster, grabbing for it with one hand while I reached for her face with the other. When I sunk my fingers into her eye, she screamed. In the next second, I heard a gunshot, but not from the one we were struggling over. I held my breath, but instead of feeling anything hit me, Fallon sunk to the ground, blood pouring from the wound that had resulted from a direct hit to the middle of her forehead.

"Sullivan!" I heard David shout as I also fell, too weak to remain upright.

He scooped me into his arms.

"I've got you. You're safe," he soothed, stroking my hair.

"This way," I heard another voice shout. I raised my head and saw Con motioning us to follow him. "It'll take us to Thistle Gate."

I rested my head against David's chest, drifting in and out of consciousness.

"It isn't much farther," I heard Con say. "Just through here." I opened my eyes enough to see him push open a door that led into a storage room.

David followed him up a few steps, then stopped and waited for him to open another door. When we came out the other side, we were in the hallway inside Thistle Gate, right across from the bedroom David and I shared.

He carried me in, rested me on the mattress, then lay beside me and held me tight to him. "You're trembling," he whispered.

"I think that's you," I said, raising my head and looking into his eyes when he cupped my cheek.

He smiled. "I think it's both of us."

"Fallon?"

"She's dead."

"I don't understand…"

David brushed my lips with his. "I don't either, but right now, I don't care about any of it. I need to hold you in my arms and feel your heart beating against mine. I love you so much."

"I love you so much too." I brought my hand to his face.

When he closed his eyes, a single tear ran down his cheek. "I've never been so terrified in my life."

"Shh," I soothed, stroking his hair like he had mine. "I'm safe. You saved me."

29

Savior

Sullivan and I slept, made love, and slept again throughout the night. Rather than impassioned, each time was gentle and sweet, a way to convey our feelings for each other and soothe what had happened without words.

As far as I knew, no one had attempted to contact either of us, and even if they had, I would've ignored them or sent them away.

"Hey," I said when she opened her eyes and looked up into mine.

"Hey." She looked over her shoulder at the sunlight streaming in through the window. "What time is it?"

"I've no idea, and I don't care."

She sighed. "I don't suppose you're going to tell me yesterday was actually a horrible nightmare."

"I wish I could, my love."

"I cannot believe Fallon was working for Weber. My God, I told her *everything*. David, she said I signed my death warrant as well as all of yours."

"We'll do everything to keep you and each other safe, Sullivan. It may mean leaving Ashcroft. It also may mean leaving the UK, at least temporarily. Whatever it takes is what we'll do."

"My mind is racing with what I missed." Sullivan groaned. "I trusted her from the very first." Her eyes opened wide. "If you hadn't stopped me, I would've given her the microSD card. At the time, it was the only place where the entirety of my investigation was stored."

"I've no doubt everyone is questioning how she was able to deceive and dupe us, myself included."

"Con in particular."

"Agreed, since I think their relationship became more than asset protection."

"She couldn't stand him."

"Another smokescreen, perhaps."

Sullivan groaned. "I'm sure you're right."

I glanced over when I noticed the screen of my mobile light up. I'd put it in do-not-disturb mode last night so I wouldn't hear calls or message alerts. When I reached over to pick it up, I saw there was only one, and it was from Gus.

Typhon and Viper ETA twelve hundred hours, it read. It was ten now, so we had time. However, we should do a debriefing between now and then.

Who's on the property presently? I responded.

Everyone.

"What's happening?" Sullivan asked.

I told her about the impending arrival and that everyone else was either already here or hadn't left.

"How are you feeling?" I asked.

"Physically, okay. Mentally and emotionally, I'm a wreck."

"Understood."

"I need answers, David. As much as I wish I could set it all aside, I cannot."

"Shall I request Gus gather everyone together at the castle in, say, an hour?"

"Please."

After offering her privacy, Sullivan said she'd prefer I shower with her. "I don't know when I'll feel comfortable being alone longer than a few minutes."

"Nor will I, letting you out of my sight for any length of time."

I sent a message to Gus, who immediately responded that everyone was already gathered in the main dining room but to take our time. He also messaged that, overnight, SIS had arranged for security to be quadrupled and the estate was on lockdown.

Forty-five minutes later, we arrived at the castle's entrance after a quiet ride from Thistle Gate. I parked, then Sullivan and I walked inside hand in hand.

"This way," I said, going left rather than right, which would've taken us toward the library. "Everyone is in the dining room." When we entered, my three closest friends stood, then took turns embracing Sullivan first, then me.

"Have you been at this all night?" I asked, noticing all were in the same clothes they'd worn yesterday.

Con spoke first. "Yes. Assessing damage and risk, primarily."

"You should know another body was found in the tunnels," said Gus.

"Whose?" I asked.

"Not yet identified."

"Dressed in all black?" Sullivan asked.

"Affirmative," Gus responded. "Wearing gloves and a ski mask. We don't have ballistic reports yet, but believe the gun Fallon was holding when we arrived on scene was used to kill him."

"He took me from the library."

Gus nodded. "We suspected that might be the case."

"Has anyone prepared a preliminary report?" I asked.

"Collectively, yes," Con responded.

"You're here," said Mairi when she walked in from the direction of the kitchen.

Both Sullivan and I stood.

"Forgive me," I heard Mairi say when the two women embraced.

"Without you, we never would've found Sullivan," I said, resting my hand on her shoulder. God knew how long it might have taken us to realize she was missing if Mairi hadn't shared her concerns about Fallon with Gus and me. I shuddered, realizing how close I'd come to losing the love of my life.

"Shall we get started?" Con asked when Mairi left the room. "The reports Ash asked about have been distributed via a secure app and should be available on your computers. We will also review them verbally."

My eyes met Sullivan's, and she nodded, then opened her laptop.

Con cleared his throat. "I'll begin with damage assessment. As we're all aware, Weber knows the extent of what we know, with a few exceptions. And those are primarily things we've learned in the last several hours." He shook his head and sighed. "Apologies, but this needs to be said. Everyone in this room is likely asking themselves the same questions I am. How was Fallon Wallace able to infiltrate SIS as well as be named editor in chief at the Crown Herald."

"Is the latter connected to the massive data breach at the news agency?" I asked.

"In part. It does appear she wasn't just hired. She was recruited into the position. University records and work experience all line up, at least on the surface."

"What do you mean?" Sullivan asked.

"All of it, including everything we think we know, could very well have been intentionally planted as well as AI generated."

I thought about Periscope's warning. It came the same day we first met Fallon. "Has any progress been made on Shelby Torriton's cause of death?"

"Typhon said he expects to hear from the medical examiner today."

"She said, 'They'll come for you. In fact, they already have.' She had to have been talking about Fallon."

"Most likely," said Gus.

If only the woman had been more specific in her warning. "She also said, 'Janus thinks he controls Chimera. He's wrong. That may be your only chance at survival.' Could it be Janus is Weber and Fallon, Chimera?"

Con typed something on his keyboard. "I wasn't able to find anything on either code name."

"Typhon was running them as well."

Something else occurred to me. "Mairi said she saw Fallon speaking with Ambrose. Has anyone questioned him yet?"

"Negative," said Gus. "What's perplexing about my mum's report is that according to CCTV, Ambrose left the estate within minutes of his leaving Thistle Gate."

"On Christmas?" I asked.

"Affirmative. However, my mum insists it was him she saw with Fallon."

"CCTV footage?"

"There's nothing after his departure on Christmas day. Nothing with Fallon meeting with someone else either."

"We need to find him."

Gus nodded. "On it."

"This means Fallon, or someone else, was controlling the fucking footage," I said, not making eye contact with anyone in the room. The fault of Fallon's infiltration did not lie on the shoulders of any one person. All of us were to blame, and I'd not have Con thinking I held him alone responsible.

"We believe that's true with Glenshadow as well," said Tag. "Which explains why we couldn't find the intruders' access points."

"The tunnels," said Sullivan.

"Come again?" Tag asked.

"They probably accessed Glenshadow through the tunnels connecting it to Ashcroft and Blackmoor."

"It's definitely possible," responded Tag. "It also stands to reason that they initially planned to abduct Sullivan, but had to abandon the plan when we discovered the perimeter breach."

"So Fallon switched her plan of attack in order to find out how much Sullivan knew and how much she'd shared with us."

"A logical line of thinking," said Tag.

"Con, you had dinner with Fallon the same night, correct?" I asked.

"Affirmative."

My head cocked. "But then, she arrived at Glenshadow the following day via helicopter."

"Again, that is correct. Since transport had already been arranged to take you to Edinburgh, I offered to have her picked up on the Isle of Arran first." Con pushed away from the table, put his elbows on his knees, and lowered his head.

"Con, don't."

"I can't help it. I actually said I believed Fallon was on the side of good, not evil. I gave you my reassurance." He got up and left the room.

"Give him a minute," I said when Tag stood to follow.

"He said it himself. Everyone here is asking themselves the same thing. How was Fallon Wallace able to infiltrate SIS?"

"I understand, Tag, and I predict there will come a time when each of us experiences what Con is going through presently. All I'm suggesting is we give him a few minutes to collect himself."

"Right. Of course. Apologies."

Less than five minutes later, Con returned. "Typhon and Viper are arriving earlier than expected. They should be touching down momentarily."

"I'll go get them," Gus offered.

After he left the room, I glanced at Sullivan's computer screen when an instant alert popped up.

"It's another message from Clive," she said. "What should I do?"

"I'd like to suggest you consider holding off a bit longer until we've had a chance to debrief further," said Con.

"Of course," she responded. "May I ask something else on the same subject?"

"Go ahead."

"Given what we know now, do we still believe my uncle has been working with Weber?"

"It's too early to say with any certainty."

"Let's take a break before Gus arrives with Typhon and Viper," I said after Con's response.

"Good idea," said Tag.

"Walk with me?" I said to Sullivan. "How are you holding up?" I asked once we were behind closed doors in a room where I hadn't set foot since my mother's death—her sitting room.

"Conflicting emotions," she admitted. "While I can mentally process that Fallon was working with Weber all along, I'm sure what I'm feeling is similar to Con. How stupid is it that one of the biggest disappointments is realizing we were never friends and she wasn't the mentor I thought she'd be?"

"Betrayal hits hard emotionally," I said, pulling her into my arms. "She positioned herself as an ally, gained our trust, and got the team as a whole to share classified information with her. Scarier still is that the woman figured out our security protocols and identified vulnerabilities."

"So much of what she said and did makes sense now, even though I didn't question it at the time."

"Such as?"

"Her interest in the tunnel systems, in particular, but also how anxious she was to stay at Ashcroft versus Blackmoor. I thought it odd that she pushed so hard to relocate, but then didn't."

"She must've had a specific reason for wanting to return to Con's place."

Sullivan murmured her agreement.

"There's something else of interest. We were joking around about how much more intelligent she was than Con. Now, I think she was giving us prompts."

"Exactly," said Sullivan. Her tone of voice and expression were more animated than they had been since we arrived at the castle earlier. "Of course she'd use prompts since it's how AI works. At least with the more simplistic apps. I mean, there are books written about how to craft a question in order to get the answer you're looking for from such an app."

From the window, I saw Gus pull up and three other people get out of the golf cart. "Who is that?" I asked, not recognizing the second woman with them.

"I don't know who any of them are," said Sullivan, turning to face the same direction I was.

"We should get back."

Rather than exit through the foyer, I led Sullivan out a different door, down a hallway, and through the smaller of the castle's two kitchens.

"I was just about to come ask if you'd like refreshments served," said Mairi.

"That would be much appreciated, especially considering neither of us ate before leaving Thistle Gate earlier."

"Of course, sir, err, David. That will take some getting used to."

"It will come with practice," said Sullivan, smiling.

"We'd offer to stay and help, but some of our colleagues have just arrived."

Mairi nudged me with her elbow and winked at Sullivan. "As if I'd allow you two in my kitchen."

We entered the dining room just as Typhon, Viper, and the mystery woman walked in with Gus.

"Before we get started, I'd like everyone to meet Dr. Margot Sterling, code name Lex, who is the preeminent MI6 expert in artificial intelligence. She'll be working with your team as the investigation moves forward."

Typhon had been looking at me, so he missed Con's expression.

"I'd say it's a pleasure to meet all of you, but under the circumstances, I'm sure you agree there's nothing pleasurable about it."

"Excuse me," said Con before storming out of the room.

"What in the bloody hell?" Typhon muttered, looking at me.

"I'll go," I offered when Tag took a step in that direction. I hurried out of the room and called out his name when I saw Con heading toward my office.

"I'm not doing this again," he said over his shoulder.

"Doing what?"

"Having someone I've never heard of, was given no background on, foisted on me. Not a chance."

"Your reaction is premature. Typhon said she'll be working with the team, not you specifically."

"Which of us knows the most about AI?"

"You, of course."

"There you have it."

"Con, I hate to say it, but I don't believe you have much of a choice in the matter."

"Don't I?"

"Outside of leaving Unit 23—wait, tell me that's not what you're suggesting."

"It's her or me."

"Can we finish the briefing before you issue the ultimatum?"

He didn't immediately answer, but when he stalked out of my office like he had the dining room, I followed.

30

Sullivan

Gus introduced me to Typhon and Viper in David's absence, after which I heard Typhon ask where he and Con had gone.

"We're all reeling a bit, sir," Gus responded.

"Understood," Viper said before Typhon did. "Sullivan, I've so looked forward to meeting you," she said, walking away from the men and approaching with Dr. Sterling.

"Err, likewise," I responded.

She chuckled. "I'd not be surprised if I wasn't mentioned. The Unit 23-ers look down their noses a bit at those of us who never left MI6. Although I will inform you that Typhon does not outrank me, as much as he might try to convince you he does."

"What she's not saying is she's the relatively new chief of MI6," Typhon said from behind her. "Which means, in seniority, I *do* outrank her."

Viper rolled her eyes. "Shall we take a seat?"

I got the impression that was more of an order than an offer, so I did.

"What I'm about to suggest may seem premature, but given the classified nature of what we'll be discussing today and in the days that follow, I'd like to extend—"

"Stop right there, Viper," said Typhon, who stood above her. "No one is extending an offer without all relevant parties present. That includes Savior and me."

"As we've just determined, I do not answer to you, Typhon."

"Ah, here they are now."

I followed his line of sight and saw David and Con had returned.

"Let's get started. I have a couple of updates. First, the ME has determined the cause of death to be poisoning from Ricin. My theory is she was exposed to it prior to the incident at Edinburgh Castle, which would also explain why she told Savior she was already dead. Any questions?"

I had several, but none relating to Periscope's cause of death, so when no one else spoke up, I didn't either.

"Next, I have some preliminary information indicating Fallon Wallace's code name may have been Chimera. I'm still waiting for my sources to confirm it. Nothing yet on Janus. While the logical assumption is it's Weber's code name, Unit 23 can't afford to act on assumptions."

When Typhon glared in Viper's direction, I nearly laughed out loud. When she stood, I held my breath.

"Prior to the start of this briefing, I initiated a conversation that was interrupted but that I need to circle back to."

"Now isn't the time—"

"Excuse me, Typhon, but I have the floor, so to speak."

He nodded once.

"While I cannot speak for Unit 23's practices, I can for MI6, and we have a serious breach of security related to classified information that must be dealt with."

Everyone in the room raised their heads, including me, who Viper turned to face. "Sullivan, I am requesting you step out."

My cheeks flushed. "Right. Of course." I closed my laptop and stood, but David caught my wrist.

"Seriously, Viper?" said David, standing. "Typhon, what's this about?"

His eyes scrunched, and he returned his gaze to Viper. "No idea."

"It's okay," I whispered to David. "I'll just wait in the other room."

"If you're leaving, so am I."

I noticed Con, Gus, and Tag stand as well.

"Hang on a minute," said Typhon, taking a step forward. "Let's not overreact."

Without another word, Con, Tag, and Gus walked out. "Let's go," said David, taking my hand.

"Look, I don't want to cause trouble. I mean, she's right about security and classified information."

"We'll speak later," David said to the three guys before leading me outside, to the golf cart.

"David?"

"I am not ignoring you. I promise." He tugged on his ear.

We rode to the cottage in silence, and once inside, David went straight to the hallway and opened the door across from the bedroom.

"Thanks for meeting us here," I overheard him say when the three men who'd left the castle with us walked into the main room.

"What just happened?" I asked.

"We have a policy in our crew. Major decisions require all of us to be on board. One dissent, and we don't do whatever it is. Or vice versa," Con explained.

"What you just witnessed was their support," David added.

"I'm confused. Why didn't you just come with us? Why did you go through the tunnels?"

"Just because it's fun," Gus responded. "They know we're here. Or at least somewhere on the estate."

"You didn't have to leave because of me."

"They did," said David, leaning closer to me. "Once I made the decision to go with you, they pretty much had no choice."

"That doesn't seem fair."

"We made a statement, Sullivan. There's a power struggle between Typhon and Viper that they need to work out between the two of them. I sensed it on our way to the castle. Typhon was not happy about Lex's involvement at this stage of the game and apparently made that clear before they boarded the helicopter," said Gus. "He obviously relented, but when Viper threw down her next gauntlet, he had enough."

I looked at David. "Did you pick up on all that?"

He grinned. "None, whatsoever."

"So anyway, now, it's up to the two of them to call a truce without the benefit of using any of us as pawns. Obviously, you mainly, Sullivan," Gus added.

"What if you lose your jobs?"

All four laughed.

"In the middle of an investigation like this one? Not a chance," said Tag.

"I hope you're right."

"Besides, removing you now, because you don't have the right clearance, is just wrong. It's also really stupid," said Gus.

"I think she wanted to offer me a job, but Typhon interrupted her."

"Thank God for that," muttered Con. "And what I mean by that is, you don't belong with MI6. If you're going to join SIS in any role, it has to be with our unit."

"What do we do now?" I asked.

Gus spoke up again. "We wait."

David cleared his throat. "But not here."

"Right. Definitely not here." Con winked and followed Tag and Gus back to the door that led to the tunnels.

"I feel terrible about this," I said once they were gone.

We sat on the sofa after he lit a fire and I turned on the Christmas-tree lights.

"Please don't. I'm glad it happened when it did. Or rather, the way it did. It's something you and I need to talk about."

"Meaning?"

"You joining SIS is something the guys and I discussed. At the time, it was premature, and maybe it still is. However, at some point, maybe even later today, I predict an offer will come. Maybe two."

"I won't pretend I hadn't anticipated the possibility. Honestly, I've already made the decision not to return to the Crown Herald."

"What are your thoughts on SIS?"

"I don't know. It would be a lot to consider. What are your thoughts?"

"I also made a decision. I'm leaving the assassination game. If there's a role for me in the unit, so be it. If not, I can live with it."

"I guess I'd have to know a lot more about what a job would entail before I could say one way or another."

David took my hands in his. "There's more to consider, and that's how we want our life together to be. I already know I can't be away from you, which is what led to my decision to resign from my current position."

"I don't want to be away from you, either."

"Not ever?" he asked.

"Not ever."

"Well, then, there's only one solution." He slid off the sofa and knelt in front of me. "Sullivan Rivers, I've loved you for over twenty years. Will you finally put me out of my misery and become my wife?"

I threw my arms around him. "Yes, David. I'd love to be your wife."

"Like the locket, the ring belonged to my mum. If you'd rather pick out something else—"

My eyes filled with tears when I looked down at the ring he slid on my finger. It fit perfectly. "I love it, David, and I love you."

We sat in the glow of the Christmas lights and the warmth of the fire, neither of us saying anything for several minutes.

"When we marry, will I become a duchess?"

"You will."

"Is there anything specific I'll be required to do?"

"Hmm. Only a couple of things I can think of."

"What?"

"First, be happy."

I thought about that for a few seconds. "You know, I think for the first time in my life, I can say that I truly am. There are still so many unanswered questions, not being any closer to finding Eric Weber or figuring out what exactly Tower-Meridian is trafficking, or whether my uncle set me up to be killed. Even with all that, I feel happy, David. Oh, I have another."

"The second requirement of being my duchess?"

"Err, no, but it is related. Once we're married, do we have to live in the castle?"

He cuddled me closer to him. "As far as I'm concerned, Thistle Gate is our home. Although that is somewhat dependent on the aforementioned second requirement."

"What?"

"The duke and duchess are expected to bear an heir, at the very minimum. How many spares we choose to have after that will determine whether we have to add onto the cottage or move elsewhere."

When my eyes opened wide, David cupped my cheek. "But know this, if you don't want children, Sullivan, I'll be blissfully happy for the rest of my life as long as you and I are together."

"Me too. And just so you know, I've never thought about being a mother. My own was not the best role model. But being with you, I can see us as parents."

"Speaking of parents, I should've considered you'd want to tell them about your engagement."

"I'm okay waiting. There is someone I want to tell right away, though."

He smiled. "Who?"

"Mairi."

"I'm surprised she isn't waiting outside the door."

"Did you tell her you planned to propose?"

"Not precisely when I would, since I didn't know myself. However, I did need her help locating the ring."

"That doesn't sound like her," I said when there was a loud knock at the door.

"It isn't." He held up his mobile. "It's Typhon, and he's not alone. Viper and Lex are with him."

"Oh dear."

"Not to worry. I have no problem putting him off for a few more hours. Say, until tomorrow?"

The man knocked again, louder. "Ashcroft, open up."

31

Savior

I groaned, stood, and let the three in.

"Where's Tag?" Typhon asked.

"No idea. He left some time ago."

Typhon shook his head. "Check your messages; he asked me to meet him here about something urgent."

Seconds later, came another knock.

"What's going on?" I asked, ushering him, Con, and Gus inside. "Tag?" I said when his eyes met mine. I'd rarely seen him so agitated.

"I received a secure message from Nightingale. All hell is breaking loose in Damascus." He turned to Typhon. "We need to get her out of there."

"On it." He stepped a few paces away, spoke to someone, then returned. "The team on the ground in Syria received an agent-in-peril alert a few minutes ago. They know where she is, and they're on their way to get her."

"Thank God," Tag muttered. "Her cover is blown, or at least she thinks it is."

"Why? What's happened?" I pressed.

"There's been a coup. The president has fled to Russia, and the rebel forces have taken control of the government."

This wasn't bad news as far as I was concerned, as long as we were able to get our people out. The president was a brutal dictator, whose family had ruled with an iron fist for half a century.

"There's more. Fearing she might not be rescued in time, she sent an encrypted file, saying it contained critical information about Weber."

"I'm opening it now," said Con, and Tag rushed over.

"Bloody hell," he muttered, looking up at me. "Con, show them."

He turned the computer around, and on the screen was a photo of Fallon Wallace, code name Chimera. Beneath the image, there was a list of aliases. The first was Eric Weber.

Sullivan gasped, and her eyes met mine. "Wait. Weber is a woman? How can that be?"

"As far as we know, no one has seen a photo before now. Right, Con?" asked Gus.

"Affirmative. And if anyone has, it was obviously not *her*."

"So who is Janus?" I asked.

Con glared up at me. "One thing at a time, Ash."

It was difficult to tell who was reeling more, him or Sullivan. Although the former made more sense since Viper and Dr. Sterling were in the room, both standing with their arms crossed.

"Typhon, a word?"

He nodded and followed me down the hallway.

"Why isn't Viper throwing a fit about Sullivan's lack of clearance?"

"Because I ran it."

"When?"

"What do you think I've been doing since you and your crew walked out?"

"Right. So, is she still considering offering Sullivan a job with MI6?"

"Nah, I shut that down."

I'd ask how, but I truly didn't want to know.

"What about you? Are you planning to bring her into the unit?"

"Of course, I'll make her an offer. Not that I expect her to accept. The job, that is. I doubt we'd be able to pry her loose from this investigation."

I took several steps until I could see her from where I stood. She was head-to-head with Con. "It appears she's already back at work."

Typhon squeezed my shoulder. "Congratulations, Savior."

"For?"

"Come on, you didn't think I'd notice the rock on her finger?"

"About that. As I told Sullivan, I'm done with the assassination game."

He smirked. "You were done the moment you didn't take the second shot. Come on, let's get back in there. We have a lot of work left to do."

"Wait. Are you really going to force Con to work with Lex?"

This time, Typhon smiled. "After all the shit he's put me through over the years? Hell, yeah. Payback is a bitch."

The following day, when we arrived at the castle, the first thing Sullivan and I did was find Mairi. Her eyes lit up when we walked into the kitchen.

"Ah, let me see!" she squealed, rushing over to take Sullivan's hand. "It fits as if it was made for you." The two women embraced, and I saw tears in both their eyes.

"I have something I want to ask you," said Sullivan, taking a step back but clasping both her hands.

"Anything, luv, you should know that."

"While we haven't had time to talk about when we'll marry or the details of the ceremony, whenever and wherever it is, would you do me the honor of standing up with me?"

Mairi wriggled her hands from Sullivan's and brought them to her tear-filled cheeks. "Aye. Nothing would make me happier, lass. You've filled my heart with joy." She looked from my beautiful fiancée to me. "As you've done too, David. I never dreamed I'd live to see the day when you and my Angus knew you were cousins."

"And that you're my aunt."

"Yes, and after the new year, I plan to inform the rest of the staff. Although, if they're anything like those who have come before them, they've already figured it out."

"I have another question. You said you saw Ambrose speaking with Fallon. Are you certain it was him?"

"Aye. I'd not mistake the man." The venom in her voice was thick.

"Do you know where he is? I've not seen him since Christmas Day."

"I am not in the practice of keeping track of your uncle's whereabouts. 'Tis bad enough he shows up here unannounced, then leaves in the same manner, locking up his suite so the staff is unable to go in and clean after he's gone."

"Surely, there's another key."

"Not that I've been given."

"I'll see that is taken care of."

"He won't be likin' that."

I shook my head. "As the castle and property were entailed to me, I don't care whether he likes it or not."

"It's about time," said Gus, joining us in the kitchen. "Brose has had the run of the place for far too long." He turned to Sullivan and motioned both of us into the dining room. "I've a request from the team."

Her eyes opened wide. "Of me?"

"They'd like to set the library up as one of two situation rooms. The other would be Ash's office."

"I don't know why I'd have a say, but I don't have a problem with it."

"Great, we'll get started."

"Wait, how is Con this morning?"

He chuckled. "Demanding Typhon run another background check on Dr. Sterling. One complete with DNA profiling."

"Speaking of DNA, are we certain Fallon Wallace was, in fact, Weber?" Sullivan asked.

"Her body was taken to the morgue in London, where collecting samples is standard procedure. The next step would be to see if there's a match in the system. Even someone who might be a close relative."

"And the deceased man found in the tunnels?"

Gus glared at me. "Rather than holding an advance briefing, how about we join the others and get to work?"

"What do you say, duchess?"

Sullivan nudged me with her shoulder. "I'm not officially yet."

"Wait. What did I miss?" Gus asked.

Sullivan lifted her left hand.

"Ah, that's very happy news. Was that your mum's ring?" he asked me.

"It was, and I love it," Sullivan responded before I could.

"Since none of the three of you noticed last night, I'd say I'm not the only member of the crew lacking in observation and investigative skills."

Gus chuckled. "Maybe not the only, but you're definitely the worst."

"Sod off, cousin," I teased.

His expression softened, but the smile didn't leave his face.

"Considering Sullivan has already taken care of this, I should too. Would you do me the honor of standing up with me when we're married?"

"It would mean the world to me, Ash."

"Good and thanks. Now, we just have to determine when and where."

"Too bad Scottish marriage laws have changed. Our ancestors would've turned up at Gretna Green and wedded the same day. I suppose you'll have to settle for the castle."

"What's this?" Mairi asked, coming out of the kitchen.

"I suggested Ash and Sullivan get married here at Ashcroft."

She clapped her hands. "Aye, it's perfect…"

I looked down at Sullivan, who beamed up at me.

"What say you?" I asked while Mairi rattled off all the plans she was already forming for decorating the various rooms, along with what food she'd serve.

She leaned up and kissed my cheek. "I love the idea, but even if I didn't, I couldn't take this away from your aunt."

As we walked to the library, I couldn't help but marvel at how much my life had changed. I'd gone from being a solitary man lost in a world where I didn't feel I fit in anywhere, who rarely visited the estate handed down for several generations, and who killed people for a living, to one who held the hand of the love of my life in mine. They may call me Savior, but it was Sullivan Rivers who'd saved me.

**Keep reading for a sneak peek
at the next book in the
Protectors Undercover Team
One series,
Undercover Infidel**

*He's the world's most brilliant
cyber intelligence expert.
She's MI6's leading AI weapons specialist.
When artificial intelligence turns deadly,
they're humanity's last defense.*

INFIDEL

I've spent my career staying three steps ahead of everyone else in the cyber intelligence game. But Dr. Margot Sterling—brilliant, infuriating, and far too perceptive—sees right through my carefully crafted defenses. When we uncover evidence that Chimera's AI weapons program goes deeper than anyone suspected, the woman given the code name Lex and I are forced to work together to prevent a catastrophe.

The problem is, I don't play well with others, especially not someone who challenges everything I thought I knew about artificial intelligence. And I definitely don't do relationships. But as the stakes get higher and the lines between professional and personal blur, I'm starting to question whether going it alone is still the smartest strategy. Especially when Sterling proves she can be just as ruthless as I am when it comes to protecting the people she cares about.

LEX

The last thing I want is to be paired with Conrad Carnegie, the infamous "Infidel" of Unit 23. His reputation for breaking rules and operating in morally gray areas precedes him. But when my research into militarized artificial intelligence reveals a threat more dangerous than anyone imagined, Con may be the only one I can trust.

As we race to contain an AI weapons system that's already gone rogue, I find myself drawn to the brilliant, dangerous man behind his carefully crafted facade. The deeper we dig, the more it becomes clear that stopping this threat will require crossing lines I swore I never would. Con's been playing this deadly game longer than anyone—I just hope trusting him doesn't prove to be my final miscalculation.

1

Infidel

The amber liquid in my glass caught the moonlight streaming in through the floor-to-ceiling windows of my private office at Blackmoor Castle.

Zero three hundred was an ungodly hour to be awake, yet every night of the last several, my eyes sprung open at the same time, with the same question racing through my mind—how had I missed the signs a woman I'd tried desperately to get in my bed, was actually the mastermind behind the development of the most potentially deadly weapons system since the atomic bomb.

That her body now lay on a cold slab in the SIS morgue did nothing to assuage the terror behind my insomnia. She hadn't been working alone and we had no leads on finding her accomplices.

I'd taken to using the hours I should be asleep to physically work my body to the point of exhaustion. Tonight was no different. After a ten-mile run on the treadmill in my gym, I was more wired than tired. I pulled my sweat-drenched shirt over my head and tossed it on the floor as I studied the endless stream of feeds on the multiple monitors set up in what I referred to as my command center, pacing between them since my constant state of anxiety kept me from sitting more than a few minutes at a time.

I poured a second glass of scotch, a rare indulgence since it only hindered my ability to sleep. After the day I'd had yesterday, I needed it. Tomorrow would be the same, knowing a few short hours from now, I'd be forced to work with a woman who infuriated me as much as just being in her presence, made my cock hard as steel.

Being forced to work with Dr. Margot Sterling, MI6's preeminent expert on artificial intelligence weaponry, was akin to a prison sentence for someone like me, mainly because I had to concede—albeit only to myself—that she was damned good at her job. There were times I'd go so far as to think she might be almost as good as I was.

I drained my drink and was headed back into the gym to do my second workout when a flash of red caught my eye.

"Bloody hell," I muttered, watching someone attempt to breach my most sophisticated security protocols.

Instead of immediately shutting them out as I typically would, I stood in utter fascination as they navigated my defenses with an elegance I'd never seen before. Their code was poetry in motion, anticipating my countermoves before I made them.

On a hunch the perpetrator wanted me to know who they were, I traced the intrusion, unsurprised to find it came from the facility I knew housed MI6's AI research division.

With a few keystrokes, I pulled up the CCTV feeds. The building appeared empty except for one office still illuminated enough that I could make out the woman behind the attack on my system. The blue glow of her monitor cast light on her long dark hair and the confident set of her shoulders. In the same way I'd sensed who my hacker was, she knew damned well I was watching.

Suddenly, every screen but one went black. On the remaining functioning monitor, the CCTV footage I'd been watching cleared and text materialized, letter by letter.

While almost as impressive as you are, your security has a fatal flaw, Lord Blackmoor.

That message quickly cleared and for a couple of seconds, a woman's face came into view. She looked directly into the camera with a knowing smirk that sent my pulse racing. Then, just as quickly, she was gone and another text animation appeared.

Your office at Blackmoor. 0900. And Con? Do have on a shirt when I arrive.

When my systems came back online as if nothing had happened, I poured my third glass of scotch, turned in the direction of the window, and raised it in a toast.

No one had gotten that far past my defenses before. The equally beautiful and dangerous Dr. Sterling would prove to be the death of me, or my perfect match. Either way, tomorrow would be interesting.

About the Author

USA Today best-selling author Heather Slade writes shamelessly sexy, edge-of-your seat romantic suspense.

She gave herself the gift of writing a book for her own birthday one year. Sixty-plus books later (and counting), she's having the time of her life.

The women Slade writes are self-confident, strong, with wills of their own, and hearts as big as the Colorado sky. The men are sublimely sexy, seductive alphas who rise to the challenge of capturing the sweet soul of a woman whose heart they'll hold in the palm of their hand forever. Add in a couple of neck-snapping twists and turns, a page-turning mystery, and a swoon-worthy HEA, and you'll be holding one of her books in your hands.

She loves to hear from her readers. You can contact her at heather@heatherslade.com

To keep up with her latest news and releases, please visit her website at www.heatherslade.com to sign up for her newsletter.

MORE FROM AUTHOR HEATHER SLADE

BUTLER RANCH
Kade's Worth
Brodie's Promise
Maddox's Truce
Naughton's Secret
Mercer's Vow
Kade's Return
Butler Ranch Christmas

WICKED WINEMAKERS
FIRST LABEL
Brix's Bid
Ridge's Release
Press' Passion
Zin's Sins
Tryst's Temptation

WICKED WINEMAKERS
SECOND LABEL
Beau's Beloved
Cru's Crush
Bit's Bliss
Coming Soon:
Snapper's Seduction
Kick's Kiss

ROARING FORK RANCH
Roaring Fork Wrangler
Coming Soon:
Roaring Fork Roughstock
Roaring Fork Rockstar
Roaring Fork Rooker
Roaring Fork Bridger

THE ROYAL AGENTS
OF MI6
Make Me Shiver
Drive Me Wilder
Feel My Pinch
Chase My Shadow
Find My Angel

K19 SECURITY
SOLUTIONS TEAM ONE
Razor's Edge
Gunner's Redemption
Mistletoe's Magic
Mantis' Desire
Dutch's Salvation

K19 SECURITY
SOLUTIONS TEAM TWO
Striker's Choice
Monk's Fire
Halo's Oath
Tackle's Honor
Onyx's Awakening

K19 SHADOW OPERATIONS
TEAM ONE
Code Name: Ranger
Code Name: Diesel
Code Name: Wasp
Code Name: Cowboy
Code Name: Mayhem

K19 ALLIED INTELLIGENCE
TEAM ONE
Code Name: Ares
Code Name: Cayman
Code Name: Poseidon
Code Name: Zeppelin
Code Name: Magnet

K19 ALLIED INTELLIGENCE
TEAM TWO
Code Name: Puck
Code Name: Michelangelo
Code Name: Typhon
Coming Soon:
Code Name: Hornet
Code Name: Reaper

PROTECTORS
UNDERCOVER
Undercover Agent
Undercover Emissary
Undercover Savior
Coming Soon:
Undercover Infidel
Undercover Assassin

THE INVINCIBLES
TEAM ONE
Code Name: Deck
Code Name: Edge
Code Name: Grinder
Code Name: Rile
Code Name: Smoke

THE INVINCIBLES
TEAM TWO
Code Name: Buck
Code Name: Irish
Code Name: Saint
Code Name: Hammer
Code Name: Rip

THE UNSTOPPABLES
TEAM ONE
Code Name: Fury
Code Name: Merried
Coming Soon:
Code Name: Vex
Code Name: Steel
Code Name: Jagger

COWBOYS OF
CRESTED BUTTE
A Cowboy Falls
A Cowboy's Dance
A Cowboy's Kiss
A Cowboy Stays
A Cowboy Wins